END OF THE LINE

MAPLE SYRUP MYSTERIES

EMILY JAMES

STRONGHOLD BOOKS

Editor: Christopher Saylor at www.saylorediting.wordpress.com/services/

Cover Design: Deranged Doctor Design at www.derangeddoctordesign.com

Published March 2018 by Stronghold Books

Ebook ISBN: 978-1-988480-18-3

Print ISBN: 978-1-988480-19-0

Large Print ISBN: 978-1-988480-53-4

For Susan. When you reach a point that you've been friends for more than half your lives, you become more like family. Thank you for always having my back no matter what life throws at us.

With lies you may get ahead in the world — but you can never go back.

— RUSSIAN PROVERB

1

I was starting to think I should have driven back to Washington, DC, to buy my wedding dress. Even though I'd never been a bride before, I suspected that my dress should fit better than it did by the fourth fitting—especially since my wedding was less than a month away.

"Don't worry." Mark's mom tugged at the side of my bodice. The large gap in the front that would have allowed me room to hide tissues—or a small cat—vanished. "We'll get them to fix this. There's still time."

She'd said the same thing when they'd hemmed my skirt two inches too long, assuming I was going to wear stilettos to my wedding, and when they sewed straps into my strapless gown. I was starting to lose faith, especially considering this wasn't the first time we'd pointed out that the bust of my dress was gaping in the front.

But Ever After was the only bridal shop in Fair Haven. A grandmother-granddaughter team owned and ran it. The granddaughter had been the one to help me select my dress, instilling confidence in me with how she helped me find a dress to fit my style.

Then her grandmother the seamstress took over. From that point on, what I wanted hadn't seemed to matter.

Mark's mom released my dress. "Wait here. I'll go talk to them."

She marched off toward the counter, where the grandmother owner rang up a purchase for another customer. Mark's mom had no daughters of her own. Since my own mom was over six hundred miles away, Mark's mom had launched herself into this wedding as if she were the mother of the bride rather than the mother of the groom. I couldn't have organized this wedding without her.

The faint tones of my cell phone ringing carried from where my purse nestled on a chair.

Mark's mom was still waiting to speak to the store owner. I grabbed the sides of my bodice to keep my dress from slipping off and picked my way carefully down from the display stand they'd had me climb onto. I had a suspicion that bridal stores used them to make brides look taller and therefore skinnier in their dresses so they'd like them better.

I snagged my phone from my purse without even stopping to look at the display.

"This is…" I started to say *Nikki*, but now that I was officially a partner in Anderson Taylor's law firm, I should get back into the habit of answering my phone more professionally. "Nicole Fitzhenry-Dawes."

"Don't let on that anything's wrong," Mark said. "I don't want to scare my mom."

A zing of pride hit me that he felt I could handle whatever was coming, then my blood felt like it pounded through my body hard enough to burst my skin. The Cavanaugh family tended to view keeping secrets as akin to treason. He wouldn't ask me to keep his call from his mom unless the consequences of her finding out would be worse than the fallout from not telling her. No, not fallout. He expected her to be afraid.

"What's going on?" I called on all my training as a lawyer to keep my tone steady and light as my words even though it was the opposite of what I felt. "We're still at the bridal shop."

"I need you to make up an excuse to leave right away and come to my place."

Voices approached from behind me—Mark's mom returning with the shop owner. I couldn't even press him for more details.

But I trusted that he wouldn't do something like this unless it was important. Had we been another engaged couple, I might have thought it was a ruse to surprise me with something good, but Mark knew I didn't like surprises. The nervous lead-up to them was rarely worth the payoff.

"I'll be there as soon as I can."

I disconnected the call, dropped my phone into my purse, and turned around, trying to act as if I'd only been checking my text messages.

"Who was that?" Mark's mom asked. She had the owner with her.

"Scammers," I blurted, then struggled to lower my heart rate and hoped my vocal pitch would follow. "Trying to tell me there was a problem with my Windows PC." I rolled my eyes. "I own a Mac."

Great. Lying to my future mother-in-law. It was a good thing I didn't believe in karma because that would have definitely earned me a black mark in return. But Mark had been insistent, and even I couldn't come up with a near-truth that fast.

"I got a call from Latvia the other day." Mark's mom made a brushing motion as if she could shoo away the callers. Her slightly amused expression vanished, and she pointed a finger at my chest, then made a go-ahead motion toward the seamstress like she would forcefully move her toward me if the woman didn't move on her own. "You can see for yourself. There's still too big a gap. It looks like she's wearing a dress that's two sizes too large."

The shop owner was even shorter than I was, with frizzy hair that she styled into almost a bulb around her head. I'd put her age at somewhere around sixty.

She pursed her lips and shook her head. "The problem is not with the dress." Her accent sounded German or Austrian. "She's wearing it wrong."

She wriggled my chest and the dress around until half of my bosoms bulged out the top. All the ideas I'd been working on for escaping from here and getting to Mark slipped out of my head as if she'd pushed them out along with my bust. I could *not* walk into my church on my wedding day with that much cleavage showing. Forget church. My bathing suit covered more skin than this.

I laid a hand across my exposed cleavage.

Mark's mom looked a bit like she was choking on her tongue. "She's practically falling out of her dress like that."

"It's sexy," the shop owner said. "That's what she's paying the big bucks for."

"That's not what she's paying for," Mark's mom said at the same time as I said, "That's not what I'm paying for."

I tugged my dress back up into the place where I, at least, thought it belonged. I didn't have time right now to argue with a woman who wanted me to look like an exotic dancer in a fancy gown on my wedding day. Mark had said I needed to hurry.

Time to channel my mom. I knew what she would say. "What I'm paying for is for you to alter this dress the way I want it to be. Until that's done, I don't need to be here."

I hiked up my skirt and headed for the dressing room. The shop owner hustled after me. One thing no one told you about being a bride was that strangers who ran dress shops would manhandle your bosoms and expect to help you dress and undress. Being a bride really should come with a warning label.

"Wait," the woman said from behind me. "I need to fit the dress."

She'd already measured twice. "My measurements haven't changed since the last time."

"Brides always lose weight before their wedding from all the stress."

I held back a snort. Escaping from a sinking car as the water closed in over us—that was stressful. Having a gun held on me—that was stressful. Being trapped in a burning building—that was stressful.

Organizing a wedding to the best man I'd ever known was

the least stressful thing I'd done in a year. In fact, not knowing what was wrong with Mark right now was more stressful than planning this wedding had been.

Mark's mom grabbed my hand. "Nikki, sweetie, it won't take long. What she really needs to do is pin your top, not take your measurements again."

Her tone was soft and overly patient, like she thought I was about to turn into a bridezilla.

That was fine. Mark had told me not to tell his mom. I'd let her think I was freaking out about the dress. The problem was, I couldn't think of a good reason not to go back and let her pin my top. If I was upset about my dress, it made sense to allow her to do what she needed to in order to fix it.

If I'd thought about it sooner, I could have made up some story about a client needing to speak to me. I couldn't throw that out now retroactively. She'd know I was making it up.

But Mark also told me I needed to leave right away. Which one would he want me to follow if I could only do one—leave quickly or hide the truth from his mom? He'd led with asking me not to tell his mom, so I'd have to assume that was the more important of the two if I couldn't do both.

I'd try one more thing to get me out of here quickly. "I'll come back tomorrow and do it," I whispered as if I didn't want the owner to hear me. "I feel like I'm going to say something unkind if I stay here any longer."

It was true enough. This woman's ineptitude made me want to say very rude things. I'd held them in and tried to be patient because I knew it was the right thing to do to be kind to her anyway.

Mark's mom patted our clasped hands with her free one. "I know, sweetie. I really do. But tomorrow you're already meeting with your cupcake baker. Besides," she lowered her voice to a whisper as well, "we need to leave her as much time to get your dress right as possible."

That was the truest statement made today.

I let her lead me back to the stand. Hopefully I'd made the right choice about prioritizing secrecy over speed.

For the next five minutes, I tried hard not to squirm. Moving would only make the task last longer. *Tried* being the key word, unfortunately. Not only were horrible scenarios starting to run through my head—like that Mark's house had burned down—but the shop owner also pricked me with every other pin. If Ever After was a place of fairy tales, she was my evil stepmother in disguise.

By the time she finished, a text from Mark waited on my phone. *How close are you?*

I left Mark's mom making our next appointment and sprinted to my car. My hands shook, and my keys rattled as I scratched them into the ignition. I forced myself to take a few deep, slow breaths before I started the car. Getting into an accident on the way to Mark's house wouldn't help anything. I sent him a message right before I put the car into gear that I was on my way.

The situation couldn't be as bad as I was imagining. If he were injured or seriously ill, he would have called an ambulance rather than calling me. If something bad had happened to someone we cared about, he wouldn't have asked me to come to his house. He would have picked me up and taken me to wherever we needed to go. In either case, we would have included his mom.

That left his house or truck. Maybe there'd been a break-in or a fire. That would be frustrating and upsetting and could make his mom worry.

He'd already moved a lot of the items he didn't need on a daily basis to my house in preparation for our wedding. Hopefully nothing he valued had been lost.

Even if it had, Mark had called me, which meant he was alright. Anything else we could deal with. Stuff was just stuff. Only living beings were irreplaceable.

I turned onto his street. Mark's truck sat parked in his driveway, but another car I didn't recognize and two police cruisers lined the street.

Since his house looked intact and there wasn't a fire truck as well, a fire was out. It had to be a break-in.

I parked my car on the road behind one of the cruisers. Two cars seemed a bit much, as well as whoever had driven the regular car here. That number of people had to be most of the on-duty officers in Fair Haven.

A chill slid over my spine like a spider made of ice had rappelled down my back.

Don't panic, Nik. He's a member of law enforcement in a sense, and the police take care of their own. That's probably why.

That had to be it. The Fair Haven police worked diligently on every case they received, but you looked out in a special way for the people who served with you.

No one was watching the front door. They hadn't even put

up the crime scene tape yet. Everyone must be engaged inside and recently arrived. Mark must have called me right after calling the police. Voices came from the direction of either the kitchen or living room. I couldn't be sure from outside the front door.

I'd find Mark and figure out exactly what had happened. He'd probably called me to have some emotional support as he filled out the paperwork for a break-in, and he hadn't wanted me to tell his mom yet because there was nothing she could do.

I passed through the entryway and into the living room.

A man's body sat on Mark's couch, in the same spot where we'd worked my Uncle Stan's case the first time he brought me here. The man's head lolled back, exposing exactly how he'd died.

Someone had slit his neck.

2

*T*he house felt like it shifted underneath me, like I was standing on a dock in a storm rather than on solid land. And I wasn't sure I was steady enough to keep my footing.

There was a dead man on Mark's couch.

My brain kept coming back to it and rejecting it as impossible. It wanted to tell me I was dreaming. Or watching a movie. That this was not real. This couldn't be real.

From my angle, I couldn't see the man's face. His build looked familiar. Intellectually I knew it couldn't be Mark. Mark texted me less than fifteen minutes ago, and based on how dark the blood on the dead man's shirt was, he'd been dead well over an hour. Besides, this man was more muscular than Mark.

But my heart wasn't listening to my brain. Instead, it felt like I'd been running on a treadmill for the past half hour.

I had to see who the man was for myself.

Because if it wasn't Mark, it still had to be someone we knew. As unreal as it seemed that Mark had a dead man on his couch, it seemed completely unbelievable that Mark would have a dead *stranger* on his couch.

I inched forward. I knew I was holding my breath from the way my chest burned, but my lungs didn't seem to want any air.

I averted my gaze from the man's wound. There was too much blood. If I looked at it, I wasn't going to make it close enough to see who it was.

One more step and I stopped and forced my gaze onto the man's face.

Troy Summoner.

Bile burned up my throat. Troy helped me find a key piece of evidence in my last case. We hadn't been friends, but we'd been learning to work together. Seeing him like this and knowing how he'd died—

"Nicole," Mark said from behind me.

I spun around. He stood near the doorway to the kitchen with two men in Fair Haven police uniforms. My brain struggled to connect names with their faces, even though both should have come easily to me.

Quincey Dornbush came into focus first. Thank God for Quincey. Mark and I were going to need a friend.

"She shouldn't be here," the other one said.

His callous tone snapped his name into place as well—Grady Scherwin.

I wanted to answer him, but my stomach refused to settle. I sprinted for Mark's bathroom.

By the time I finished losing the breakfast I'd had with Mark's mom a couple of hours ago, Mark joined me in the bathroom. He handed me a damp washcloth and sat next to me on the bathroom floor.

I wiped my mouth. It would be a long time before I could also wipe away the image of Troy with his neck slit from my mind. If I ever could. Some things stayed with you forever. "What's Troy doing in your house?"

It wasn't exactly the right question, but it was as close as I could get to asking why Troy was dead in his house. Mark and Troy weren't friends, either. They didn't socialize. Troy shouldn't have been here even alive. Especially not so early in the morning.

"I don't know." Mark's voice carried a strange, strangled note, like he knew how that sounded.

My last client gave me a similar answer when I'd asked him what happened. He'd told me he didn't know whether or not he'd killed his employee, and he blamed his medical condition. "You don't have sporadic fatal insomnia, do you?"

My own voice had a riding-a-rollercoaster-for-the-first-time panic to it.

Mark shook his head and opened his arms. I leaned into his hug.

"I'm glad you're finally here," he said.

He'd called me because he needed me. I had to pull myself together. He already had a dead man on his couch. He didn't need a passed-out woman on his bathroom floor. "Am I here as your fiancée or your lawyer?"

"A little of both."

I could be his fiancée later. Right now, it seemed he might need a lawyer more. And I could handle this situation better in lawyer mode anyway. "Do you have an alibi for Troy's time of death?"

"I don't know when he died. We're still waiting on the medical examiner from the next county."

Right. That was a stupid question on multiple fronts. Obviously, he wouldn't know the time of death. If he knew the time of death, that would mean he was here when Troy died, and he likely would have known why Troy was here.

He wouldn't be allowed to examine Troy's body as the medical examiner since he'd be a person of interest in Troy's murder. There was no way given the manner of death that this could be an accident, which was probably why so many officers had responded.

The bathroom floor was cold, but I wasn't ready to go back out to where Troy was—partly because seeing him there made my chest ache for him and his family and partly because I was a selfish person. Seeing him there reminded me what I had at stake here. Troy wasn't just dead. He was dead in Mark's house. Mark, who I loved and was supposed to marry in less than a month.

A less selfish person wouldn't look at Troy's body and see the potential consequences for their own wedding and future.

I wasn't a less selfish person, though, and I'd wanted to be a normal bride who could focus on her wedding and her groom rather than on dead bodies and murder. Just once, I wanted to be normal.

I shifted position to get more comfortable, my back against the sink. There was barely room for both of us to sit side by side. At least the floor was clean. I'd never been more grateful to Mark's cleaning lady.

I linked my hand with Mark's so he'd see I was with him even though I wasn't looking him in the eyes anymore. "How about you tell me what happened?"

Mark let out a long huff of air as if he'd forgotten to breathe until that moment. "I got a call early this morning to head out to an accident right at the county boundary. When I got there, no one else was there. No accident. No people. I called in, but I was at the right place. Dispatch didn't know what had happened, so I headed back. When I got home, I found Troy. My door was still locked and there wasn't any sign of forced entry."

Someone had set him up. They'd drawn him away on a fake call, so they could bring Troy to his house and murder him, effectively framing Mark. Dispatch would be able to confirm that they'd called Mark, but if I were the prosecution, I'd argue Mark set up the fake call himself to provide an alibi.

"Did you stop anywhere along the way? Did anyone see you?"

Mark shook his head.

With no witnesses and no one at the location he'd gone to, he had no way of proving he'd actually gone.

Thankfully for us, whoever worked Dispatch last night would be able to tell us who called in the accident. The person trying to frame Mark wouldn't have been stupid enough to use their own name or officer number when they called it in. Hopefully, though, they wouldn't have thought to disguise their voice. If the dispatcher could identify them by their voice, we'd have a solid lead for who was behind this.

Until then, I had to do everything possible to protect Mark from whoever set him up. "Were you questioned?"

Mark nodded.

"What did you tell them?"

The look he gave me said *isn't it obvious?* "The truth. What I told you."

To him it would seem obvious. He was innocent, so he answered whatever they asked. When the police considered someone a potential suspect in a murder, though, it was never that simple. Unless we could prove he hadn't been involved, the police would dig into his life with the intent of finding guilt.

Mark probably wouldn't believe that if I told him, though. He was used to being allied with the police.

Quincey would believe Mark and wouldn't try to trick him, but their friendship meant Quincey would quickly be replaced. Even Chief McTavish might not be allowed to conduct this investigation. At least I was here now to monitor the rest of the questions.

I climbed to my feet, dropped the washcloth into his sink, and moved for the door. "Then what we need to do is figure out why someone would want to frame you for Troy's murder."

Mark clambered to his feet too fast to be graceful and shifted to the side so he was in front of the bathroom door. He placed a hand over the knob.

At first I thought he planned to open it for me. But his hand stayed in place and the door stayed closed, preventing me from leaving. His Adam's apple struggled up and down in his throat.

Like he had something to hide. Like there was something he wasn't telling me.

My throat felt blocked, as if I'd tried to swallow something much too big. For a second, it was like I wasn't standing in front of Mark anymore. I was standing in front of my dad, who controlled when a conversation started and when it ended. Who controlled how much I knew about any situation we were involved with—including hiding from me that he'd known all along my boyfriend was guilty of murdering his wife.

Or like I was standing in front of Peter, listening to him lie to me, telling me he hadn't killed his wife. And I'd believed him—not because he was the world's greatest liar, but because I *wanted* to believe him.

Mark hadn't been in a situation like this before, but I had. If he turned out to be guilty too, it would destroy something in me that I was sure could never be fixed. Not everything broken could be repaired, and not everything was stronger after you repaired it. My faith in humanity and my own judgment certainly weren't stronger after Peter broke them.

I rubbed a hand around my throat. "What's going on?"

He cupped my face in his hand and ran his thumb across my cheek bone. "I know I called you here, but you can't investigate this."

That sounded awfully guilty. What reason could he possibly have for not wanting me to search for the truth unless he knew the truth and didn't want it coming out?

"Don't you think we should do everything we can to prove you didn't do this?"

"Chief McTavish will be here any minute. He'll believe me, and he'll find the real killer. But you can't be involved."

McTavish and I hadn't always agreed on who the guilty party was in a murder investigation, but he had proven that he cared about finding the truth, and he was a good police officer. He wouldn't charge someone with a crime simply to have an elevated closure rate or to satisfy the press.

That said, my parents had taught me not to leave something important to anyone else. You delegated the tasks where mistakes could be fixed or wouldn't matter in the long run. You delegated tasks when you could hire someone with a higher degree of skill. You didn't delegate the things that really mattered when you were the one who could best complete the task.

I couldn't navigate unless I had a GPS telling me where to go, and my cooking wouldn't be winning any competitions, but as Liam Neeson's character said in the movie *Taken*, I did have a very particular set of skills. When it came to proving Mark's innocence, I trusted my skill set over Chief McTavish's. I knew my strengths.

But Mark knew my strengths, too. As much as I wanted to, I couldn't come right out and ask him why he was arguing with me on this. The only two reasons I could come up with were that he didn't believe in me as much as he said he did, or I couldn't believe in him when he said he didn't do this.

Had he actually said he hadn't done this? Crap. I couldn't remember, and I couldn't ask if he'd already told me without letting him know I had doubts. But hadn't he only said he'd found Troy? He hadn't said he'd found Troy dead. That could be implied or intentionally left out.

Focus, Nic. Don't give ground. The truth is too important. "I'd feel better if I was investigating this as well."

Mark's hands slid down to my shoulders, and he squeezed almost too tightly. The panic sensors in my brain flashed on.

He loosened his grip. He glanced back over his shoulder even though the door was closed, and last I knew, he didn't have x-ray vision to see through the wall to what was going on beyond it.

He turned back and held my gaze more tightly than he'd held my shoulders a moment before. "Troy's dead in my living room."

The laugh lines at the corners of his eyes had deepened into something else—fear lines.

Sometimes my desire to investigate a puzzling case overcame my common sense. This wasn't about Mark wanting to hide anything from me. It was about Mark wanting to protect me from a dangerous situation I'd been trying to run straight into. I should have seen that sooner. I might have if history hadn't come back in to crush me under its massive weight.

Troy, a man we both knew and worked with, was dead in his home. Unlike most people in Fair Haven, Mark locked his door, a remnant of his time living in New York City. To get in, they'd have either had to pick his lock or have stolen his key and made a copy of it without his noticing.

A shiver ran over my body like I'd jammed both hands into a bucket of snow.

Whoever had done this was skilled. He was deadly. And he was targeting Mark.

If I went after the killer, it'd put a bigger target on me than I'd ever had before.

I was willing to take that risk for Mark.

"Promise me you'll stay out of this," Mark said. "Please, Nicole."

The use of my full first name cut off every argument I'd been planning to make. I didn't need all the fingers on one hand to count the number of times Mark had called me Nicole since learning I preferred Nikki.

However we dealt with the situation, it had to be as a team. Investigating it against his wishes would only pit us against each other at a time when we most needed to stay united. And I wouldn't truly be helping him if fear for my safety destroyed all his peace.

"I don't like it, but I promise."

4

I spent the evening on the Internet studying lock picking just in case Mark changed his mind and I got a look at his doors. We'd need to figure out how someone had gotten in.

Working around Sugarwood the next day and then going to my meeting with our cupcake designer rather than investigating Troy's death left me feeling like I was showing up to an appointment on the wrong day. On the drive there, I'd come up with a list of reasons why Mark couldn't have been serious about asking me to stay out of the case and why I should ignore him even if he had been. With every turn, I talked myself into and then out of investigating anyway.

But every time I decided to secretly investigate, I remembered the look on his face, and I knew how I'd feel if I asked him not to do something and he did it anyway—willfully, despite knowing how important my request was to me.

It'd feel like a betrayal, and I couldn't let Mark down that way. I might not agree with him, but I had to respect his wishes in the same way I expected him to respect mine.

I parked my car beside Isabel Addington's cupcake food truck, How Sweet It Is, in the Lakeside Park parking lot.

Isabel and How Sweet It Is showed up in Fair Haven just as the summer tourist season came to an end. She'd only been passing through, planning to stay a couple weeks at most, but I'd begged her to stay long enough to create a cupcake display for my wedding. I hadn't been able to find anyone around who could make the maple syrup cupcake I'd been imagining. The first bite of Isabel's cupcakes had assured me she could do it.

It'd taken the promise of a big bonus and calling in a few favors to have other friends ask her to also cater their events, but she'd finally agreed. We'd been meeting semi-regularly in the past six weeks as she worked on perfecting the recipe she was designing specifically for me.

I stepped out of my car, and the cold sliced straight through my coat and gloves as if I wasn't wearing any. Hopefully Isabel had cranked the heat in her truck. If she hadn't, I'd subtly drop the hint that we should meet at her home next time. There was no reason for her to bring her truck all the way out here. Even the winter tourists weren't going to the beach in this weather.

The food truck's door popped open before I could knock, as if she'd been watching for me.

I stepped in, and she locked the door behind me.

My shoulders tensed as if someone had suddenly turned my veins to iron. Locking that door felt like it was meant to keep me in rather than to keep others out. There wasn't anyone else out there.

The hyper-logical lawyer part of my brain could hear how irrational that sounded, but the half that was still reeling from Troy's death didn't want to listen.

"Do you have many people walk in on you as if you're a normal store?" I tried to keep my voice light, as if I wasn't sure how a food truck worked rather than that I thought she might be about to kidnap me.

Something flitted across her face that I couldn't interpret. She tugged the door. "Not yet, but I guess that'd be another good reason to lock up. It's an older truck. If I don't keep it locked, it lets in a draft."

My metal-stiff shoulders eased. That made more sense than the crazy conclusions my brain wanted to jump to. Isabel might have met Troy—I'd gotten most of the police department hooked on her cupcakes—but I couldn't think up an obvious reason she'd want to kill him. A romantic affair seemed unlikely. She looked to be in her late thirties, almost old enough to be his mother.

Besides, her answer seemed reasonable. The air inside the truck was so warm it was almost too thick to breathe. Definitely not drafty with the door locked. I slid off my jacket and set it aside.

Isabel still wore her puffy silver jacket with the hood up. The hood squished her black hair around her face, and her lips and cheeks were red from the cold, making her look a little like the painted face of a Russian nesting doll.

She rubbed her gloved hands together. "Is it always this cold in Michigan in the winter?"

I held back a snort. If it was, I might have to reconsider my choice of home. This was only my second northern winter. It was already colder than the first, and we weren't even into January yet. "They keep promising me these temperatures are record-breaking. I'm not sure yet whether they're lying to me or not."

"I'm going to hope whoever told you that wouldn't lie to you," she said with a smile.

Isabel's smile was like a firecracker. When she wasn't smiling, I would have described her as average-looking, but when she smiled, it was a bit like those gossip pages where they showed pictures of celebrities with and without their makeup side by side. I might not have recognized her.

My phone vibrated in my pocket. I snatched for it, praying it wasn't bad news from Mark. The display showed Russ' name.

Technically I didn't need to answer it, but if he'd heard about Troy's murder, not answering would panic him. He'd assume something had happened to me.

"Go ahead and answer," Isabel said. "It'll take me a minute to set the cupcakes out."

I slid my finger across the screen and answered.

"You're not working Mark's case." Russ' tone made me imagine him pounding his meaty fist into a table. "I forbid it."

I guess there wasn't an *if* involved. He'd heard about Troy's murder. Thank you so much, Fair Haven gossip chain.

The first response that jumped to my lips was to tell him he couldn't forbid me from doing anything. Even at Sugarwood, we were co-owners, and I had the controlling share. It wasn't like I was a child and he was my dad.

I swallowed all those responses down. Russ had been going to grief support group meetings with Stacey and me, and had been making progress. Before the cold hit, he'd even started walking with Mandy and my dogs to lose some weight. He still tended to be blind to his personal triggers, though. The main one seemed to be fear he'd lose another person he loved. When baby Noah came down with a cold, he'd forced Stacey to go sit in the ER for hours, only to have the doctor tell her to give him some Tylenol to bring down his fever before sending them home.

Snapping at him for caring about me didn't seem to be the right response even if his approach came straight out of a previous century. "Mark and I decided to leave the investigating to Chief McTavish this time."

"Who'll defend him?" Russ asked. His tone clearly said *I don't believe you.*

"He hasn't been charged with anything yet. *If* he needs someone to defend him, my parents will do it. And Anderson offered to go with Mark if they bring him in for further questioning until my parents get here." Anderson had sounded almost giddy about the prospect of working with my dad, right up until he seemed to remember what that would mean for Mark and me.

Russ harrumphed, but he ended the call. Maybe I should turn my cell phone off. Gossip in Fair Haven was as inescapable as gravity.

"It's ready when you are, Nicole," Isabel said from behind me.

I must have been standing and staring at my phone for longer than I realized if she needed to nudge me. I pocketed my phone and sat at the tiny table she'd managed to squeeze into the space between her counters while I'd been on the phone.

I could already feel extra heat creeping up my neck at what she might have overheard. Add that heat to the warmth in her truck, and I'd be close to passing out. Time to redirect attention somewhere else. "You can call me Nikki. Do you prefer Isabel or Izzy?"

She glanced down at the cupcakes on the table and rearranged them. "Either's fine."

The way she said it made me think she'd never considered it before. Anyone who had a name that could be shortened to a nickname thought about it. Most people I knew had a strong preference. Unless it wasn't her real name.

Which was more than a little paranoid. Maybe I should talk to Mark again about me building a defense for him should he need it. Every shadow I saw was going to turn into a monster under the bed otherwise. My brain apparently couldn't know a murderer was in Fair Haven without trying to find them.

The sugar from Isabel's cupcakes was much needed. The way I felt right now, I might have cupcakes with a chaser of candy bars on the way home.

I'd tested the tiramisu cupcake and was unwrapping the maple syrup cupcake when my phone rang again.

If it was Russ calling back, he could go to voicemail this time. Him warning me off the case would only make me want to take it on even more.

This time the display read *Mandy* instead. I gave my maple syrup cupcake a longing look and Isabel an apologetic one. Mandy had a tendency to keep calling and texting incessantly until she got an answer. "A member of my wedding party."

Originally, Mark and I had planned to keep our wedding

party to his two brothers, my best friend Ahanti, and Elise. Once Elise married Erik, though, Mark felt he should include him, but once he included him, it felt wrong not to ask Quincey, who'd been Mark's friend longer than Erik had. To balance things out, I asked Stacey—Sugarwood's assistant office manager—since she was like a little sister to me, and Mandy. My mom's reaction of *But she's in her 60s* hadn't dissuaded me. Mandy and I had been through a lot together. The days she got on my nerves were far outnumbered by the days she'd come through when I needed her.

Isabel waved for me to take the call.

"Is Mark okay?" Mandy asked after a rushed hello. "I heard they arrested him."

Just when I thought the Fair Haven gossip mill couldn't get any worse. "They didn't arrest him."

"But they found a dead man in his house."

Thankfully it sounded like the Fair Haven police officers at least knew how to stay quiet. Mandy didn't know who had died. It might even be the real reason she called.

I gave myself a mental kick. That thought didn't do Mandy justice. She liked hearing gossip, but only because she liked to speculate. She didn't spread it around. The identity of the dead man would be less interesting to her than how he got there and why.

Still, I had to squash even the idea that Mark was guilty. "You had a murder in your B&B. That didn't make you a murderer."

"Someone must be trying to frame him, then. I bet it's an ex-boyfriend of yours trying to stop the wedding."

My only ex-boyfriend had at least twenty-five years left on his prison sentence. I could guarantee he wasn't behind this.

"How is this going to affect the wedding?" The speed of Mandy's words made me think she'd been talking while I'd been thinking and I'd missed some of what came in between.

"It's not. Chief McTavish will figure out what happened, including that Mark wasn't involved, and the wedding will go ahead as planned."

Mandy's pause felt like the silence between a lightning flash and the thunder, full of nervous anticipation over how loud it would be. The cupcake I'd just eaten lay heavy in my stomach.

"I thought someone would have told you," Mandy said. "Chief McTavish is missing."

*A*s I disconnected the call with Mandy, I reminded myself that her source also told her the police arrested Mark. They could be wrong about McTavish as well.

Please, Lord, let them be wrong about Chief McTavish.

Right or wrong, I wasn't going to be able to concentrate on cupcakes until I knew.

I wiggled out of my chair. "Something's come up. Could you pack me a few samples and my fiancé and I can try them together?"

Isabel stayed in her chair for a full ten seconds, then rose to her feet slowly. Like she was buying herself time to make a decision.

I'd gotten the impression that she had a narrow margin of profit on her truck. She was probably doing the math in her head to figure out if she could afford to give me extras for free or if she needed to ask for money. Even though she was putting together the cupcake tree for my wedding, it didn't mean I should take advantage of her and eat up extra products she could otherwise sell.

I reached for my purse. "I'll pay you, obviously."

Isabel held out her hand in a *stop* gesture. "Don't worry about it." She lowered her hand to her side, but her fingers tapped a barely noticeable beat on her leg. "Is everything...Are you okay?"

There was something in her voice, like she was asking me something deeper than the actual question. I just wasn't sure what it was.

And as nice as she seemed, I didn't know her well enough to share the whole strange affair with her. She overheard enough already.

"Everything's fine. It's just a case I'm working."

I needed to be careful. This lying thing was getting out of hand.

She nodded, but it wasn't an *I believe you* nod. It was an *I'm accepting you don't want to talk about it* nod.

She packaged up two of each of the flavors. I'd already decided I wanted a maple syrup cupcake, but Isabel suggested we offer at least three options. Not everyone liked maple, she said. The other contenders were tiramisu, cookies and cream, white chocolate raspberry, and lemon meringue pie. I'd told her I didn't want the traditional chocolate and vanilla, so she'd suggested some of her most popular cupcakes as options.

She passed the cupcake carrier to me, but didn't meet my gaze. "There are people who can help if you find you're in a situation and don't know how to get out."

She said it quietly and casually, as if she were saying *Make sure to try them all.*

It took a second for it to click in my brain what she meant. She thought that Mark might be a danger to me.

I tucked the cupcake carrier securely into my body. "It's not what it probably sounded like. My fiancé wouldn't hurt me or anyone."

Isabel unlocked the door and gave me the same nod she had before when I'd told her everything was fine. "Be sure, okay? They call them red flags for a reason."

INSTEAD OF CALLING MARK, I DROVE STRAIGHT TO ELISE AND Erik's house, where Mark was staying until the police released his home. We needed to find out if what I heard about Chief McTavish was true. And if it was, I didn't want him to be alone when he heard the news.

I turned onto Elise's street at almost the same time as another car turned into the driveway. A woman wearing a Fair Haven police uniform, her dark hair pulled back into a tight bun, stepped out of the car. Elise.

In the middle of the day. Driving her personal vehicle rather than a police cruiser when she should be on duty.

There was no scenario in which this was a good thing.

I sped up and swerved into a spot in front of the house before Elise could reach the door. My tire scraped along the curb, and Elise spun around. She came down one step and waited.

I stopped in front of her without climbing the steps.

She smoothed both her hands over her already-smooth hair. "What are you doing here?"

Elise had always struggled to hide her tells. The fact that she asked me what I was doing here was a dead giveaway that she didn't want me to ask what she was doing home in the middle of the day. She'd have been less obvious if she'd simply assumed I was here to see how Mark was doing.

I'd been right to assume that her coming home now wasn't good. "I heard Chief McTavish was missing."

Elise's shoulders slumped, but it looked more like relief than shame to me.

"I don't know how much time we have," she said, "but I'm glad you're here."

The tendril of hope that Mandy's information had been wrong withered and died. Elise hadn't denied that Chief McTavish was missing.

I'd at least been partly prepared for it. Her response, though, suggested she wanted support for whatever had brought her home.

I braced a hand against the railing. "How much time we have until what?"

"Until they come to arrest Mark."

Her voice dropped to a whisper, as if she somehow hoped I wouldn't hear her. Or maybe she didn't want Mark to overhear.

Either way, she had to be overreacting to Chief McTavish's disappearance. Unless they'd found some irrefutable evidence that Mark was involved with his disappearance—and they couldn't have that—they shouldn't be arresting him for anything else yet. Yesterday, Quincey seemed certain that someone was trying to frame Mark, and he'd expected that to be the direction the investigation took.

"What makes you think they're coming to arrest Mark? Quincey—"

"Quincey isn't running the investigation. Neither is Erik. I'll explain inside."

Elise retreated up the stairs and opened the door for me. It wasn't until she offered to take the cupcake tray from me that I remembered I was holding them. I didn't have an appetite for them now.

Mark came around the corner and stopped. His gaze jumped back and forth between us, landed on the cupcake tray, then came back up to our faces. "I'm guessing this is about something more serious than a problem deciding between the cake flavors."

Elise laid the cupcake tray on the bench by the door where they hung their coats. "Chief McTavish is missing, and I've been temporarily relieved of duty. Erik, too. Erik's still at the station, making calls and trying to reach whoever made the decision, to reason with them, but he doesn't think it'll help. Things have gone too far. We're all under suspicion."

She waved us farther into the house. Once in the living room, she actually drew the curtains closed. Under any other circumstance, her old-movie cloak-and-dagger air would have struck me as funny, but it felt like I'd forgotten my sense of humor in the car. Or, more accurately, back in Isabel's food truck when Mandy told me Chief McTavish had gone missing.

"They've sent in outside investigators," Elise said. "All Fair Haven officers are banned from accessing anything to do with this case. Quincey's still working, but they've sent him on traffic duty. They didn't directly say so, but it seems like they think we either helped Mark commit the murder or we'd tamper with evidence to let him get away with it."

Crap. No, double crap. And even that wasn't strong enough to express what this meant. The courts might operate under *innocent until proven guilty*, but the police didn't. Quincey and the other Fair Haven police might have made an exception with Mark. Outside officers wouldn't, which was likely why they'd been brought in.

Mark stood in the middle of the room, rubbing the stubble on his chin with one hand. The fact that he hadn't shaved today spoke volumes about his emotional state.

I slid my hand into his and squeezed until he looked down at me. I waited for him to focus on me. "We'll fix this. Other than Troy being in your house, they don't have any evidence against you. My parents have won cases with ten times more concrete evidence than that against their client."

Elise was smoothing her hair again, like even one strand out of place would cause the rest of her to go to pieces. "They have more evidence."

I knew my head was shaking, but it felt like I watched it happen from the outside.

"They can't have evidence." It was Mark's voice speaking, but he said what I'd been thinking. "I didn't do this."

"I know that." Elise's words came out sharp and loud. "But they do."

The snap in Elise's voice reminded me too much of what often happened between clients and their families when dealing with a criminal charge and having to mount a defense. Tempers grew short, doubt crept in, and isolating the ones who cared about you most became much too easy to do. Many relationships didn't survive a criminal trial, even when the defendant was declared not guilty.

I'd found the kind of family I'd always longed for in the Cavanaughs. I wanted to marry Mark, but I wanted to marry *into* his family as well. I refused to allow this to destroy them.

Besides, Elise had made it sound like they could be coming to arrest Mark soon. We didn't have time to waste bickering amongst each other. We needed to know what we were up against. Then we needed to prepare an explanation for whatever they thought they had against him. It couldn't be conclusive evidence. There'd be holes.

I held Mark's hand tight and reached my free hand toward Elise in a placating gesture. "We're all in agreement that Mark didn't do this. What evidence are they claiming they have?"

I picked the word *claiming* intentionally. It didn't accuse any individual officer of lying, but it also made it clear that I believed they couldn't possibly have any real evidence against Mark.

Elise drew the curtains tighter and flicked on a lamp so forcefully it wobbled. "They found a burner phone in the back of Mark's bedroom closet. It had a text to Troy's phone the night Troy died, saying *Meet me at my place.*"

My legs suddenly felt as stable as melting wax, and my vision went blurry at the edges.

Mark let go of my hand and sank into the nearest chair. He rested his elbows on his knees and buried his face in his hands.

Elise had stopped talking, which was good, because I wouldn't have been able to hear her over the buzzing in my ears.

A lawyer doesn't panic, Nicole, my mom's voice lectured me over top of it all. *Panicking loses cases.*

And for the first time, I was glad my parents had drilled their teachings into me so thoroughly that I still heard them when they weren't around. I had to pull myself together and be lawyer Nicole. Lawyer Nicole was strong. She could handle this.

"Were there fingerprints?" My voice still sounded thready and far away.

Elise shook her head. "Wiped clean."

Too bad it didn't have the real murderer's fingerprints on it, but whoever planned this was too smart to leave their prints behind. Wiping it clean, in my opinion anyway, still suggested the phone didn't belong to Mark. He wouldn't have had any reason to wipe down his own phone, especially if he also intended to hide it. I knew that was the argument my parents would make if he were their client. And it sounded like he soon would be.

I knew better than to ask how Elise got the information. The outside investigators hadn't been entirely wrong to place her on leave. Before they had, she'd obviously been digging into the case when she shouldn't have been. She would never have done anything illegal the way they suspected, but it wouldn't be the first time she'd pushed the lines to help someone important to her.

I rested my hand on Mark's back. He hadn't looked up yet. "The killer could have planted it after killing Troy," I said.

Elise's eyes looked watery, like she was trying not to cry.

Oh no. "There's more, isn't there?"

"They found the scalpel used to…"

I could almost hear the words *slit Troy's throat* teetering on the edge of her tongue. Thankfully, she seemed to want to say them as little as I wanted to hear them said.

"Used to kill Troy," Elise continued, "in the trash can by the road, like Mark was hoping it'd be collected before the police found it."

There could be only one reason that would make Elise fight tears when the cell phone hadn't. The words hurt coming out of my mouth. "It had Mark's fingerprints on it."

6

*M*ark's back muscles shuddered under my hand, and Elise stared at me.

Maybe I was wrong. Maybe I was wrong and her stare meant she was shocked I'd even suggest it. But I couldn't assume anything.

I straightened. "Elise, did the scalpel have Mark's fingerprints on it?"

She nodded once, quick and sharp.

That was going to be hard for even my parents to explain away in court.

It was hard for *me* to explain away.

Maybe you shouldn't be trying so hard, the annoyingly logical voice in my head said. *Look where that got you with Peter.*

Breathing became enough of a challenge that I had to order my body to draw in air and let it out again. I sent up a quick prayer for wisdom. I needed more than I had on my own.

I'd wanted so much to believe Peter hadn't killed his wife that I'd blinded myself to the truth. I'd promised myself I'd never do that again. But love did funny things to people. Could Mark have done this, and I was repeating my history?

Something twitched in the back of my mind, like a mental muscle spasm. The fingerprints didn't make sense. "It's backwards."

Mark sat up slowly. The hard lines around his mouth softened slightly. "You still believe me?"

The words of my last client, Clement, when I'd suggested his wife tried to kill him came tumbling back into my mind. *You have to believe in the person you're spending your life with.*

I rocked back. Mark hadn't been upset because of what the police found. He'd been upset because he thought he might lose me, lose my faith in him. My belief in him mattered more than what could happen in the court. He knew what it meant for us if I didn't trust him.

Mark wouldn't do something that could cost him our relationship. He'd proven that to me.

There was only one reason he would have killed Troy. Troy would have had to be actively trying to kill me so that Mark had to kill him first to stop him. That hadn't been the case.

And I knew in a way I'd never known with Peter that Mark hadn't killed Troy.

I leaned in and kissed him. "I believe you. I know you wouldn't have done this."

He leaned his head back into the chair. "Thank God." He rubbed his hands over his face one more time, then sat up. "What did you mean by *It's backwards?*"

The change was almost jarring. As long as I still trusted him, he could believe there might be a way out of this, despite how condemning the evidence was beginning to look against him.

And that, maybe more than anything else he'd ever said or done, made me feel like I was something special.

"What's backwards?" Elise echoed.

Right. Focus, Nikki. You'll have plenty of time to think about your relationship once it won't be through prison bars.

"If the cell phone belonged to Mark and he hid it and planned to keep it, but the scalpel is what he killed Troy with and he was trying to dispose of it, he would have wiped his prints off the scalpel and not the cell phone. The only reason for it to be the other way around is that they somehow stole a scalpel that already had Mark's fingerprints on it. They couldn't get his prints on a phone the same way."

Elise pulled the curtain aside and let it drop back into place. "That won't be enough to convince the investigating officers that he didn't do it."

Probably not. "They don't have motive, either. Unless they want to argue that Mark's a serial killer, they need motive."

Elise peered out the crack between the curtains now. She had to be watching for the other officers so we had warning, but didn't want them to know so it didn't make Mark look guiltier.

"Grady Scherwin"—she said his name like it was a curse word —"told them about you throwing up when you saw Troy, and they started asking whether you'd ever thrown up at a crime scene before. It sounds like they think you were cheating on Mark with Troy, Mark found out, lured him to his house, and killed him."

"And then called it in. Do they think he's stupid?"

"They think he's guilty, and they're going to explain away anything that hints otherwise."

Mark pushed to his feet and stepped between Elise and me, his back to her, blocking her view of us. "I think we need to postpone the wedding," he whispered. "This might not be resolved before then, and it's not fair to you to marry me if I'm going to end up in prison for the next twenty-five years."

I couldn't argue with his logic. My parents might well advocate for the same thing once they found out. But I didn't want to lose Mark any more than he wanted to lose me. There wasn't another Mark out there. "I don't care if they put you away for life. I still want to marry you, and I'll spend all my time filing appeal after appeal until you're free."

He leaned his forehead against mine. "Thank you for believing in me."

"Thank you for not believing I was cheating on you with Troy."

"I know you better than that."

There was almost a smile in his voice, like he was thinking back to the conversation we'd had right before our first kiss. We'd barely begun dating and a crazy man with a vendetta against me had tried to make it look like I was cheating on Mark. He'd said those same words to me then.

"And I know you better than to believe you'd murder someone," I said. "We'll figure this out together, and we're getting married as planned."

Elise said something under her breath that sounded like a real curse word this time. "They're here."

My heart jolted like it came loose in my chest. I'd been hoping she was wrong about the police coming for Mark. Elise did tend to be melodramatic at times. I should have known, though, that she wouldn't have scared us like this if she wasn't certain.

I wrapped Mark in a hug. "I'll call Anderson. He'll meet you at the station. Don't say anything to the police except that you want your lawyer."

He didn't argue this time or act like I was silly to suggest he not answer any questions. He didn't even question me calling Anderson. Anderson wasn't going with him because I doubted myself this time. He was going with him because of the role the police thought I'd played in this.

The doorbell rang. Elise cast one glance in our direction and headed for the front door.

Mark held me so tightly it was almost hard to breathe.

"I should go meet them at the door," he said, "so Elise doesn't have to show them in here and feel like her home's been violated."

Even now, he thought of everyone else first. Elise. And me, wanting to keep me safe.

The time for protecting me, at least, was over. "I want to investigate this and help build your defense. With Chief McTavish missing and someone intent on framing you, I don't think we can leave it in the hands of the police."

Mark's chest raised high enough that I felt the movement against my body. "I hate to say it, but you're right."

The adrenaline rush I usually got when faced with the puzzle of a new case didn't come. Instead, all my bones felt too heavy for my body to carry, like fear had infused itself down to my marrow. Of all the cases I'd been a part of, this was the one I could least afford to lose.

Male voices carried from the front of the house alongside Elise's. I didn't recognize either of them. In a way, it was a small mercy. I wasn't sure I could have handled it had they sent Grady Scherwin.

Mark must have heard them, too, because he let me go. He pressed a gentle kiss to my lips. "Just be careful. I'd rather go to prison for the rest of my life than have anything happen to you."

---

7

*E*lise and I sat side by side on her couch after the officers took Mark away and I'd called Anderson, my head on her shoulder and her cheek resting against my hair. I always used to like the smell of her green apple shampoo, but I had the uncomfortable feeling that, in years to come, whenever I smelled that scent, I'd now think of this moment. Though the memory wouldn't be entirely bad. Yes, Mark had been arrested, but I hadn't had to face it alone. I'd had Elise with me, and I'd been able to call Anderson for help.

Anderson had told me to stay away from the police station for now. Given the depth of the frame-up, he wanted as few moving pieces as possible. It wouldn't be the first time the police told a suspect a lie about their spouse or loved one to trick them into confessing. If I wasn't there, they couldn't use me against Mark.

I'd told Anderson I'd start working the case while he did

what he could for Mark, but so far all we'd done was sit on Elise's couch and stare at the wall. My body felt numb.

"I don't understand why anyone would do this," Elise said in a similar tone to what I imagined someone would use if they came home to find their house or car vandalized—a little angry and a lot like they couldn't fathom someone destroying something valuable simply for the sake of it.

I didn't understand it, either. Most people liked Mark. We couldn't possibly have a big pool to draw from for people who'd want to hurt him.

Elise lifted her head. "You don't think the chief..."

I didn't blame her for not being able to finish the thought. The timing for Chief McTavish's disappearance was more than a little suspicious. He'd either had something to do with Troy's death or he'd become a target as well.

I didn't know which to hope for. On one side, he'd have tricked us all into believing he was a good and honorable man when he wasn't. On the other, the odds were good that he was dead.

"How do we know he disappeared?"

"They couldn't reach him, and his wife said he was gone when she woke up." Elise touched the spot where she carried her cell phone. "They pinged his cell and found it in the snow next to his car. His keys were still there too, like he'd just walked away and left it all behind."

I was almost afraid to ask my next question. "Where?"

Elise dropped her head back down onto mine. "The parking lot for Lakeshore Park."

If Isabel and I had met there one day earlier, we might have noticed his car. That likely wouldn't have changed the outcome, though. I didn't know his personal vehicle well enough to recognize it, and if he'd been in a cruiser, I probably wouldn't have thought anything of it sitting there. I'd have had no reason to report it, and Chief McTavish's disappearance wouldn't have been discovered any sooner. I couldn't have helped spare him.

"Mark would have driven right past on his way to the nonexistent call," Elise said quietly. "That's also bad for Mark, isn't it, that McTavish went missing?"

A good prosecutor could spin that so many ways. Chief McTavish was Mark's accomplice in the murder, and Mark killed him once Troy was dead. Chief McTavish figured out that Mark was planning to kill Troy, tried to stop him, and Mark killed him, too.

None of the possibilities played favorably for Mark.

I'd have to come up with an equally viable alternative for why the two things happened on the same night. "Maybe Mark and Chief McTavish worked a case together, and a family member of someone they sent to prison wanted revenge on both of them."

Elise's head moved in what I could only imagine was a shake. "You've worked most of the murder cases since Chief McTavish came to town. They'd have targeted you, too. And Mark doesn't usually present the condemning evidence. I could see someone wanting revenge on a police officer who put the evidence together, but Mark deals in facts—time of death and cause of death stuff."

"Maybe the killer originally planned to follow Mark outside of town, and Chief McTavish was driving by, and..."

And I had no idea where I was going with that, it was so far-fetched. I was starting to sound like Mandy, throwing half-baked spaghetti-ideas at the wall.

Elise did me the favor of letting my tangled idea die a quiet death.

I sat up, bringing Elise with me. We couldn't afford to skip steps or jump to conclusions. "Let's go back to the beginning. We're assuming this was about someone framing Mark as a way to hurt him. Could it be about someone wanting to kill Troy and cast the blame somewhere else?"

The way we'd been sitting had loosened one side of Elise's hair. Her sixth sense must have picked it up because she method-ically released her hair and swept it back into a neat bun again, holding the bobby pins between her lips as she worked.

She jammed the final pin in. Cousin Elise disappeared and cop Elise took her place. "If it was about Troy, why choose Mark? They weren't even friends. There had to be easier places to kill Troy and easier people to frame for it."

We could ask the same if it was about Mark. Why choose Troy? Neither Mark nor I had wanted to say it to each other, but I would have been the obvious choice had someone wanted to hurt Mark.

Elise's bookshelf full of framed photos caught my attention. Most of them were of Arielle and Cameron growing up, but she also had shots of her and Erik, her parents, Mark and me with my dogs, Megan and Grant with their kids, and the whole Cavanaugh family gathered together at Thanksgiving.

I wasn't the only more obvious way to hurt Mark. The killer would have had any number of obvious choices if they wanted to hurt Mark. Sending him to prison wouldn't hurt him as much as taking away someone he loved.

Unless it wasn't about hurting him.

I turned back toward Elise. "You said Mark deals in facts. It could be that someone was trying to discredit him or prevent him from testifying in an upcoming case."

Her hand went to her hair like she was considering pulling the pins out and starting over again. "It wouldn't work. The prosecution could still use his results even if he couldn't testify, and framing him for murder wouldn't call into question the results of his autopsies."

Too bad stomping my foot would have been childish. It would have helped release some steam.

Elise raised her hands and shrugged her shoulders. "I don't know how we're going to get anywhere. We don't have enough to go on."

We didn't. We needed more information, and the obvious place to start seemed to be with whoever had called in and had Dispatch send Mark out into the middle of nowhere.

8

Since Elise could get fired for looking into Mark's case further, we decided she'd go break the news about Mark's arrest to the family while I tried to contact the dispatchers.

Elise kept apologizing like I'd given her the easier task. I was too much of a coward to tell her that explaining everything to the Cavanaughs felt like the much more difficult, scarier job. My parents had prepared me to weasel information out of people. They'd taught me to manipulate. They hadn't taught me how to gently break hard news.

My time would be much better spent trying to find out who called in the fake accident.

I didn't want to go home to Sugarwood to make the calls, where I might run into someone who'd have questions I also wasn't prepared to answer. Or who'd try to talk me out of what I was about to do—like Russ.

Elise said I could stay in her house. Arielle and Cameron still had hours left in the school day.

Thanks to my close association with most of the Fair Haven PD, I knew the names of the four regular dispatchers/desk officers. I prayed one of them was on duty the night Troy died. If someone had been out sick, it'd be harder to track down an out-of-town fill-in, and someone who wasn't a regular might not have recognized the voice of whoever made the call.

Unfortunately, I only knew one of the dispatcher's phone numbers. Sheila and I took our dogs to the same obedience classes back when Velma was a puppy. In between classes, we'd met a couple times to practice together.

I scrolled through my saved contacts and pulled up Sheila's number. The call went to voicemail. I opted not to leave a message. Somehow *Hey Sheila, were you the one on duty the night Troy died?* didn't seem like the kind of thing you should leave on a recording.

Since she wasn't answering, she was likely at work. I keyed in the number for the police station's front desk.

Sheila answered.

"It's Nicole," I said.

I wouldn't say anything more until she responded. That would tell me how much she knew about Mark. Hopefully she was up-to-date, and I wouldn't need to explain the situation before asking for her help.

"How are you?" Her voice was low enough to let me know she wasn't completely alone, but she also didn't have anyone standing over her shoulder at the moment. "This place has gone crazy. It wasn't even this bad after the Chief Wilson fiasco."

I'd gone back to Virginia to pack up my belongings after former Chief Wilson went to prison for murdering his wife and my Uncle Stan. I was too busy grieving Uncle Stan, tearing my old life apart, and being conflicted because I thought Mark was married to consider the chaos I left behind in the police department. They'd all come under scrutiny then as well because of the corruption that Chief Wilson had been covering up. Chief McTavish had been sent to Fair Haven not only to replace him, but also to make sure the corruption ended with the removal of Chief Wilson.

"I'm managing." Sheila had always been skittish talking about work. She used to evade my questions when I'd asked how her day had gone when we were in obedience classes. I didn't want to spook her by coming right to my point. Thankfully, she'd opened the door a little by saying the department was in chaos. "Were you working the night it happened?"

"I'm on days now. I didn't even find out about Troy until I came in this morning."

I couldn't imagine what that must have been like. She'd come in thinking she knew what to expect from her day—she might deal with tragedy, but it'd be tragedy at a distance. She wouldn't have expected to walk into it on a more personal level.

"It's surreal," she said. "Let me know if you need anything, okay?"

Even though it was a social nicety and she probably didn't expect me to take her up on it, it was an opening I was going to charge into. "Could you tell me who was on that night and give me their phone number?"

"Nikki." The way she said my name had a plea to it.

She wasn't going to tell me.

"I hope you understand," she whispered, "but I can't."

I could understand. She still had her job. That was more than could be said about nearly half the Fair Haven police force at this point. And it might not even be about her job. It might be an ethical thing for her. She might simply not feel right about sharing information with me about an active case. Lawyer or not, I was also Mark's fiancé. Anderson was the one on record as Mark's lawyer, not me.

None of that rationalizing took the sting out of it, though.

"You'll be in my thoughts," Sheila said. Her voice went up on the end, as if she expected that to make her refusal easier to bear.

Being in someone's thoughts was about as useful as owning a pair of shoes you never wore.

And then she hung up on me before I could pressure her. Which was probably a smart move on her part. Despite her plea for me to understand, I would have pushed her to give me some sort of direction at least.

Now I was back to trying to find the phone numbers of the other three dispatchers on my own.

Fair Haven still produced an old-fashioned physical phone book—I'd seen it back when I stayed at The Sunburnt Arms. Elise should have a copy. If she didn't, I'd try searching online, but an online search could yield so many results that I'd have to make a lot of wrong number calls before actually finding the people I wanted.

Her copy of the phone book turned out to be underneath the base for her house phone. It was also five years old, so she either threw the new one out by accident or Fair Haven changed so little they didn't feel the need to produce a new phone book more than every five years. Given what I knew of the town, my guess was the latter.

I took it with me to the kitchen table. Only two of the remaining dispatchers were listed. The first one I called wasn't on duty the night Troy died. He had heard about Mark, though, and he made sure to tell me he didn't believe he'd done it.

It gave me a much-needed boost before I called the next dispatcher. Case Hammond was friends with Grady Scherwin. While Grady seemed to respect Mark, I'd stepped on his toes one time too many. I'd even gotten him replaced with Troy when my dogs were kidnapped because I didn't trust him to do a thorough job investigating. Case had surely heard all about it, including some choice terms for me.

I dialed his number anyway. I didn't have a choice. Our only lead at present was whoever called in the false accident.

A man answered without giving his name.

Without asking, I could only assume I had the right person. I certainly wasn't going to jump into my request without being sure.

"Is this Case Hammond?"

"Whatever you're selling, I don't want any."

The call dropped.

He must have thought I was a telemarketer. I clearly needed to work on my professional phone voice if I sounded like a scam artist.

I redialed. This time he didn't answer. Lovely. He recognized my number from before and was taking the ignore-the-call tactic

I often took when I got repeat calls from a number I knew was trying to sell me something or swindle me.

I hung up and grabbed Elise's house phone. I dialed again.

"Hello," the same male voice said.

I was going to assume it was Case since he hadn't said *no* when I asked for him before. Had it been the wrong number, he would have told me so rather than basically telling me to shove off.

"This is…" Maybe I shouldn't tell him my name. He might be more willing to help me if he thought I was working with Mark's lawyer. It wasn't a lie, either. Anderson and I were partners. "I'm with Anderson Taylor's law office. We're representing Mark Cavanaugh. I'm trying to reach the dispatcher who was on duty the night Troy Summoner was killed. Am I speaking to the right person?"

There'd been music in the background before, like he'd been listening to the radio. The sound cut in half. "Sorry, say that again."

I repeated it, leaving out my name and praying that he wouldn't notice.

"I wasn't on that night."

His tone suggested Mark didn't have a chance if we were his lawyers and didn't even know how to contact the right person.

I grabbed up the phone book and ruffled the pages near the phone so it would sound like I was looking through papers. "Are you sure? The information we got from the police lists your name. Case Hammond."

"I was on the day shift." Now he sounded a bit like he wasn't sure whether he was the one I was looking for or not. "But I didn't talk to Cavanaugh. I think he probably called 911, and that goes to a central county dispatch. I answer calls that come into the Fair Haven police station."

That was all information I already knew, except that Case had been working the day shift that day.

But maybe I could get the other piece of information I needed. I hadn't had much interaction with Case, but I had with Grady, and people tended to befriend others like themselves. Grady was hyper-macho, like he belonged in a past era. Maybe sounding a little flustered would trigger a *rescue the damsel in distress* feeling in Case. If he assumed the police gave me his name and number, he shouldn't see anything wrong with giving me Henry McCloud's number.

"I'm so sorry. Your name and number were the ones I was given." I added a little extra fluff to my voice, trying to imitate an airhead secretary from old black-and-white TV shows. "Do you know who was working that night? My boss is going to be angry if I don't get the information he wanted."

By process of elimination, I already knew who was working. But what I didn't have and couldn't get without his help was the phone number.

Be the hero, I silently urged him.

The music in the background vanished. Case had either turned it off or left the room. "Everyone wants to see Cavanaugh found innocent of this, and it sounds like you made an innocent mistake. I was working the day they investigated the murder. Makes sense they gave you my name by accident. Let me get you the number for Henry. He's the one I replaced when I came in."

I wrote down the number as he read it off, dutifully

repeating it back. I wouldn't get another chance if I wrote it down wrong.

After he hung up, I set Elise's phone down on the table and stared at it. Other than hanging up when he thought I was a telemarketer, Case had actually seemed nice. Whether he would have been as helpful had I been honest with him about my identity was up for debate, but he'd wanted to make sure Mark got the best chance at a good defense by helping his lawyer's office with the right information.

The man still had abysmal taste in friends, but no one was perfect.

Now I had to pray that Henry would be less reticent to share information than Sheila had been. He didn't *have* to tell me anything.

My first interaction with Henry McCloud was when I'd called the station trying to reach Quincey Dornbush during my first month living in Fair Haven. Because Henry fondly remembered my Uncle Stan, he offered to get Quincey's phone number for me. On the surface, that should make my chances good that Henry would help me.

The only problem was he'd still followed protocol getting me Quincey's number. He'd radioed Quincey first and asked permission. Whether or not he helped me now could depend on whether he felt I had a right to the information. That all hinged on whether he saw me first as Mark's lawyer or first as his fiancée.

Thankfully, Case hadn't had the same concern over giving out Henry's number or I would have had to devolve into hanging around in the police station parking lot, waiting for him to come into work.

I dialed the number Case gave me. It rang for the third time. If he didn't answer, should I leave a message? It seemed even less wise to leave one for him than for Sheila.

"McCloud," a man's voice said.

I jumped. I'd been so busy thinking about whether to leave a message that I'd stopped paying attention.

"This is Nikki," I blurted.

That sounded too much like Mark's fiancé and not enough like his lawyer.

"Nicole Fitzhenry-Dawes," I said in my professional tone. It might need work, but it was all I had at present.

"I thought you might be calling me." There was a smile in his voice like he found my amendment of my name humorous. Like I hadn't fooled him at all, and he guessed why I'd done it. "Are you officially Mark's lawyer? You know I can't discuss details of an active investigation with you if you're not."

The way he said it made it hard for me to tell if he was gently instructing me to lie to him. As long as I told him I was Mark's lawyer—whether it was true or not—he'd talk to me.

This time I couldn't lie, though. Henry wouldn't get in trouble for my lie—which might be why he nudged me in that direction—but I'd have crossed into something borderline illegal. That wasn't a line I ever wanted to cross. Mark wouldn't want me breaking the law for him.

Thankfully, even though Anderson might be lead on the case, Anderson and I were partners. That did make me Mark's lawyer in some capacity. I might be batting my eyelashes at the line of legality, but I wasn't letting it take me home.

"Mark is represented by my firm."

"What would you like to know?" Henry asked. His tone still carried that smile, as if he saw my choice of words for what they were as well.

I could understand why that would strike him as funny, but his amusement felt slightly inappropriate. Someone he'd worked with had died, the chief was missing, and Mark stood accused of murder. I'd always been described as cheerful, and I was struggling with smiling these days.

But everyone dealt with stress and loss in different ways. If the past year had taught me anything, it was that.

"I know you were the one working the night Troy died. What we need to know is who called in the fake accident Mark went to."

"It was Troy." The humor was gone from Henry's voice now. "Troy made the call."

9

*M*y chest went tight, like I'd fallen and knocked all the air from my lungs.

If Troy made the phone call that drew Mark away from his house, we'd be back to having no leads.

It was still an *if* though. I was going to run this case using everything my parents had taught me, and that meant no assumptions. Double-check everything. Leave no chances for the prosecution to disprove your arguments. "Are you sure it was Troy? Could it have been someone else using his name or badge number?"

"It wasn't just his name or badge number. It was his voice."

The desire to both throw something and cry built inside of me. I couldn't do either. The first would be childish, and the second wouldn't solve anything. Well, except for releasing some frustration. "Could it have been someone impersonating Troy's voice?"

"They'd have had to be world-class. I hear all the officers' voices so often that they can't fool me when they try."

On any other day, the idea of Fair Haven officers trying to play a practical joke on one of their dispatchers would have made me laugh. Now it simply mocked me and the fact that our best lead for proving Mark's innocence had evaporated.

The longing to cry pushed out the desire to destroy something. Elise and I hadn't considered Troy might have made the call. It was the worst possible outcome. "After Troy called you, you called Mark?"

"I did."

I guess at least we knew Troy was alive when Mark left home. How that might help us, I wasn't sure, but I'd take whatever I could get. "Did you also call Chief McTavish?"

Elise had mentioned that McTavish was gone when his wife woke up. Something must have happened to get him to leave his house. A phone call or a text like Troy received seemed the most likely. Elise hadn't said there was a useful text found on Chief McTavish's abandoned cell phone, so I was betting it'd been a phone call. If we could cross Dispatch off the list, that meant the last number who called his phone might be another lead.

Henry coughed a few times. "Sorry, the cold I had a month ago won't give up." He cleared his throat a couple of times. "I called the chief. Before I called Mark, I think. Troy said the accident looked suspicious to him. With a fatality involved, I thought the chief would want to go."

I planted a hand over my mouth to keep from groaning out loud.

That made it look like Mark had kidnapped or killed Chief

McTavish as well as Troy. The prosecution would argue that Mark forced Troy to make that phone call to Dispatch. I could think of at least ten better ways to create an alibi for myself if I wanted to kill someone than faking an accident call, but my opinion didn't matter. Once this went to court, only the jury members' opinions mattered. All the prosecution had to do was say Mark was smart enough to figure out a way to both give himself an alibi and lure Chief McTavish out to the middle of nowhere.

"I'm sorry I couldn't be of more help," Henry said. "Mark's a good guy, and it's terrible this had to happen to him."

"Thanks anyway."

I disconnected the call before I lost control of my tear ducts. I'd hung so much on being able to crack the story of the person who placed that call. Now I knew Troy had placed the call that sent Mark out that night, but not much more.

I straightened in my chair. That wasn't entirely true. I knew one other thing. Troy said the accident looked suspicious, which meant the medical examiner would need to be sent out. But he hadn't asked for Chief McTavish to be sent as well. Henry did that on his own. It was possible McTavish was the collateral damage in all of this.

The person who forced Troy to make the call had expected Mark. Maybe he'd planned to ambush him and kill both him and Troy. If McTavish arrived before Mark, the killer would have had to change his plans.

I pressed my palm to my forehead and pushed my chair back from the table. Elise and I assumed this wasn't about a case Mark worked with Chief McTavish and Troy because all the major cases McTavish had worked since coming to Fair Haven, I'd been involved with as well. I hadn't been targeted.

Taking McTavish out of the equation meant taking me out of it as well. There could have been a case that only Troy and Mark worked.

I had to reach Mark. He could give us a list of cases that he'd worked with Troy. There couldn't have been many that Troy played a major role in. He was a junior officer. Those might be able to be narrowed even further if Mark could remember anyone making a threat or reacting in anger.

Hopefully Anderson was still with him at the station. I sent a text instead of calling. If the police were still questioning Mark, Anderson wouldn't be able to answer a call.

My phone rang a second later.

"They charged him with Troy's murder," Anderson said in lieu of a hello. The additional static on the call told me he was already in his car. "Since it's already Friday, the best we could do for a bail hearing was Monday morning."

Mark would stay in the Fair Haven holding cells until then rather than being moved to a regular jail somewhere, but that was a small comfort. He didn't deserve to be locked up for even one night.

It also introduced an additional problem. With Anderson gone, he couldn't ask Mark my question. And I definitely didn't want to put this investigation on hold over the weekend. The longer we waited, the easier it would be for the real killer to cover his tracks. The police wouldn't be looking for anyone else anymore. They thought they had the killer. With most of the people close to Mark placed on leave, he wouldn't even have anyone there advocating for them to consider other options.

"How far away are you?" I asked.

"I know I should have called you right away, but I'm going to be lucky not to be late for court as it is."

Not what I'd meant, but it answered my question none the less.

"I did call your mom," Anderson said. "I figured it was time to bring in the heavy hitters. We have a conference call with your parents scheduled for tomorrow to go over everything we know so far."

Perfect. That meant I'd be getting a call or text from my mom imminently asking why she had to hear about this from Anderson. I'd have to do damage control on that later.

Right now, I'd have to go to the station myself and ask Mark. The trick would be convincing the officers there to let me see him.

10

The Fair Haven police station smelled like wet wool, and someone had turned up the heat higher than Chief McTavish ever allowed the thermostat to be set. It reminded me a bit of Isabel's food truck. Whoever was in charge now had probably grown up in a more southern state.

Sheila looked up from the front desk and hunched down as if she didn't want me to see her. No doubt she thought I'd come to press her for more information.

The vindictive part of me wanted to let her squirm for a bit because she'd been unwilling to help me, but that wasn't the kind of person I wanted to be.

"I'm here to see Mark," I said as soon as I got close enough for her to hear me.

She planted her elbows on the desk, and her shoulders relaxed backward. "I'll call someone for you."

I went over to what I called the Yearbook Wall. Each year,

the Fair Haven police station took a photo with all the employees, framed it, and hung it on the wall in the lobby. It looked like they'd been doing it since the inception of the department, but I couldn't tell for sure because the oldest photos hung far above my head. Only the ones from the past twenty years were at my eye level.

I liked to study them when I came in. It was fun to see how long each person I knew had been here, to see the changes in hair styles, and even watch the long-standing members age.

I'd been in this station more often than anyone but an employee should be. Not only when investigating cases, either. I'd come to drop something off to Elise, or to meet Erik for coffee, or to bring samples of some new maple syrup treat that Nancy, my employee who had a gift for baking and candy making, was experimenting with. It wasn't only Mark who had friends here. They'd become my friends as well.

It felt different today, almost like I'd come home to find someone had redecorated my house while I was at the grocery store. Sheila's face was the only familiar one, and I still felt the distance her refusal to help me had created between us.

I went over to the metal bench along the wall to wait instead and shifted my gaze to the floor. It was too unsettling to watch so many strangers milling about, none of whom had a space in the photos on the wall.

"Are you the one who asked to visit Mark Cavanaugh?"

The man's voice sounded like it belonged to an opera singer —deep and rich.

I looked up. The voice didn't match with the person standing in front of me. He looked to be around fifty, wasn't much taller than I was, and had cheeks so red they looked like he'd painted them with blush. He'd also spilled coffee on his striped gray tie at some point today.

He put a hand over the stain as if he'd caught me looking. "Cavanaugh isn't allowed visitors until after his bail hearing."

I rose to my feet. My dad always said you were more likely to get what you asked for if you weren't negotiating from a position of weakness. That included psychological cues of weakness, like being on a lower level than the person you were speaking to.

Even if they weren't allowing regular visitors, they still had to allow Mark access to his legal counsel.

"I'm not a visitor. I'm his lawyer."

His hand moved off the stain, as if he were no longer worried about what I might think. "I met Cavanaugh's lawyer. Unless you've had a sex change in the past hour, you're not him."

It might have helped my case if I was dressed more professionally, but I hadn't planned on doing case work when I'd picked out my clothes this morning. I'd only planned on eating cupcakes, and my favorite jeans and a fuzzy sweater worked great for that.

"I'm co-counsel with Anderson Taylor. He was called away to court before we could finish discussing the upcoming bail hearing with our client."

The officer raised both his eyebrows. He clearly thought I was lying.

What I wouldn't give right now to be able to ask for Chief McTavish. Did I even have a business card with me?

I held up a finger in a one-moment gesture and dug through my purse. My parents were probably flinching all the way from Virginia that I didn't have a card holder to keep business cards where I could easily find them. In my defense, it wasn't like I was actively sourcing clients. Since I only worked with people who claimed to be innocent, any work I received would come through Anderson.

But he had printed up business cards with both our names on them and he'd given me a whole stack. Most of them were still in the box on my kitchen counter. I was sure I tucked a couple in my purse to show Mark's mom, though.

A little white corner peeked out from the middle of two grocery receipts. Bingo.

I wriggled it out and handed it over, praying he wouldn't notice the badly bent corner. "I can produce ID if you're still not convinced."

He looked at the card and then tapped it against his palm.

There shouldn't have still been a hesitation. Unless—crap. He recognized my name, but not as a lawyer. Elise had said something about them thinking Mark killed Troy in a jealous rage over me.

I imagined the way my mom's face looked when she was dealing with a particularly confrontational officer. "Is there a problem Detective...?"

"Dillion." He tucked my card into his suit jacket pocket. "Whether or not there's a problem depends on whether you're lying to me right now."

Bending the truth, yes. I wasn't here because Anderson ran out of time. Lying, not exactly. I was working Mark's case. But I knew how to play the game. If I tried to defend myself, I'd only look guiltier. "What benefit could I possibly get from lying to you about being Mark Cavanaugh's lawyer? Unless you believe I'm here to break him out." I held out my arms. "You're welcome to check me for weapons if you'd like."

I made sure to let a touch of derision slide into my tone. It left a slimy feeling in my mouth after the words were out. Posturing might work for my parents, but it always felt wrong to me, like I was trying to fit into someone else's clothes.

He turned and motioned for me to follow him. "I'll show you the way." He glanced back over his shoulder. "But you can only have ten minutes. There's no reason you should need more than that to prepare your client for a bail hearing. Assuming he's not considered a flight risk, you'll have plenty of time to discuss anything else regarding the case after that."

I let the *flight risk* zing pass with a smile. If I jumped to Mark's defense, it would only call into question my professionalism. "Thank you. Ten minutes will be more than enough."

The sidelong glance he leveled at me turned my hands cold. It was a look that said he didn't believe attempting to break Mark out was actually outside of what I was capable of. It was a look that said they'd be investigating me almost as closely as they were investigating Mark as they continued to build the case against him. It was a look that said they had no doubt he was guilty. And that I might have helped him plan this whole thing.

I kept my mouth shut through the rest of the walk. Had it been anyone else who walked me down, I might have tried to dig a little. But the part of me that had years of experience as a lawyer watching police officers work said, this time, I'd lose more than I'd gain if I did.

We reached Mark's cell. He shot to his feet. He opened his mouth, then closed it again. He'd probably been about to ask me what I was doing there. Thankfully he'd figured out just in time that I'd end up kicked out of the station without what I'd come for if he did.

I gave Detective Dillion a pageant-worthy smile. "I can find my way back up. You don't have to wait for me."

He pulled up his sleeve enough to reveal his watch and touched one finger to the face—an unspoken reminder of my time limit—then he turned and left us alone.

I couldn't help rolling my eyes. "He's almost as bad as having to work with Grady Scherwin."

"Scherwin seems to be one of the only officers they haven't put on leave. I saw him when they brought me in."

That figured. The only officers who didn't have some sort of good relationship with Mark were the ones who were either both new and young—like Troy had been—or were kind of unpleasant—like Grady Scherwin. It was a small pool, and it left us without allies on the force when we could most use them.

"I'm guessing you didn't come here to talk about Scherwin, though," Mark said.

I almost made a joke about how I missed him already and snuck in for a kiss, but just thinking the words brought an uncomfortable burning sensation to my eyes. I explained my guess about this connecting to a case he and Troy worked together.

Mark blew out a long breath. "That's going back over a year. If we had access to the case files, that'd be easy to figure out."

"If I'm right, it'll be a case where someone wasn't happy with the results."

"I worked a drunk driver case. He got off on a technicality, but that had nothing to do with me. I only dealt with the body of the person he killed." He pinched the bridge of his nose. "And I can't remember if Troy worked that one with me or not."

Mark usually had an exceptional memory. I'd heard stories of how he could answer questions in court without consulting his notes. He barely needed to refresh his memory.

But the pressure of testifying in court as a professional wasn't the same kind of pressure a person felt when they were behind bars, fighting for their own freedom and knowing that everyone was looking at them and wondering if they really did the horrible thing they were accused of.

The pressure of only having ten minutes—five now—didn't help.

"Come at it sideways." I used the same soothing voice that worked to coax my bullmastiff Toby when we went to the vet. "Have you personally received any threats or angry messages?"

He brought his hand away from his face. "One. He wasn't threatening, but he was angry. I deemed a death natural causes, but the man's son was convinced his stepmother killed his dad for his life insurance policy. He called for weeks and even showed up a couple of times asking me to reconsider. I had to have him removed from the funeral home, even."

It was possible someone who felt justice hadn't been

rendered for his loved one could move from angry to vengeful. "Was Troy involved in the case?"

Mark shrugged his shoulders. "I can't remember, but he was the one who escorted the man out of Cavanaugh's and told him, if he didn't stop, they'd hit him with a restraining order."

The door at the end of the hallway swung open. Time was up. Dillion was back.

I yanked my phone out. "What were the names?"

Mark told me in a hurried whisper. With Dillion coming toward us, I didn't even get a chance to squeeze his hand before saying goodbye.

He'll be out on Monday, I reminded myself. *He's not a flight risk, and we'll find a way to make whatever bail they set.*

In the meantime, I'd call Hal, the private investigator I'd worked with on a few prior cases, and have him look into the names Mark gave me.

As I was dialing Hal's number on my way to my car, a text came into my phone. I stopped to check it.

Isabel.

Were you able to narrow it down to a couple favorites?

I leaned against the door of my car, keys in one hand, phone in the other. It might be paranoia and nothing more, but Isabel's behavior still struck me as odd. It wouldn't hurt to have Hal dig into her background as well.

Troy and Chief McTavish were both fit men who'd been trained to defend themselves. For both of them to be overpowered by a stranger seemed like a stretch. They wouldn't have turned their back on a man they didn't know if anything at all seemed off about his behavior. They also wouldn't have been relaxed enough to allow a man they didn't know to pull a gun on them. They'd have reacted, and we'd have found signs. They'd have had their guard up with a strange man.

They might not have if their attacker was a woman.

And Isabel had been in the area of Lakeshore Park around the time McTavish went missing.

11

I debated whether I should wear a nice blouse for the conference call with my parents, right up until I figured out that we probably wouldn't have video on our call. I put the blouse on anyway. My parents always seemed to know things they shouldn't, and I wanted this to be a conference among equals. I didn't want us sidetracked with anyone thinking they needed to coddle or protect me.

Especially after the conversation I'd had with my mom last night. I'd expected her to be angry at me for not calling her immediately, but instead she'd sounded worried about both Mark and me. Worry wasn't something I normally heard in my mom's voice. In fact, I'm not sure I could ever remember hearing it before.

I got to Anderson's office ten minutes early. To his credit, Anderson kept the fan-boy gush out of his voice as he updated my parents and me on everything the police asked and tried during the interrogation. He clearly laid out the evidence they had against him.

"Have you considered arguing self-defense?" my dad asked, his voice matter-of-fact. "We could make a decent case for Troy luring him out of his home in order to rob him. Mark came back earlier than Troy thought, a shadowy figure attacked him, and he defended himself with the nearest object."

I scowled at the handset. My dad couldn't see it, but it made me feel slightly better.

I leaned closer to the phone so he couldn't act like he didn't hear me. "We're not arguing self-defense because Mark is innocent."

I made sure my voice had no emotion. I didn't want to give my dad any ground to suggest I shouldn't be part of this or that I was irrational and my opinions should be ignored.

"They're never innocent, Nicole. You of all people should know that by now."

It was an echo of the conversation we'd had in his office after I figured out Peter was guilty of murdering his wife. His words to me then had been *They're always guilty.*

I wanted to hang up on him. I wanted to remind him of how much he'd respected Mark prior to this moment. I wanted to remind him that I'd worked with many innocent people since coming to Fair Haven.

I wanted to do a lot of things, but I couldn't do any of them because I needed my parents on this case. Whether I liked it or not, they were the best at what they did. One of them had more experience than Anderson and me combined. My pride wasn't more important than Mark's freedom.

Anderson cleared his throat, breaking the dead air that'd hung since my dad's statement. "There weren't signs of forced entry or a struggle, and I'm not sure we could convince a jury that even a doctor would have a scalpel lying around his house. If the victim were killed with scissors or even a kitchen knife, it'd be a lock."

My dad made a statement about how he'd convinced juries of more ludicrous things and that it was all in the way we sold it.

But all I could hear was that he wanted to argue self-defense because he thought Mark was guilty.

It was exactly why we needed to not only win in court, but also prove who had done this. Mark shouldn't have to spend the rest of his life with people looking at him crossways the way they did O.J. Simpson. Mark was innocent.

"Mark's not Peter." My words came out louder than I intended.

It wasn't until after they were out that I realized I'd talked over someone.

Muffled voices came from my parents end of the line, like one of them had covered the handset.

Anderson shifted in his seat as if he didn't know who to stick up for—his idol or his partner. "Who's Peter?" he whispered.

I motioned that I'd fill him in later. Hopefully he'd forget.

"I'm...sorry, Nicole." The edge had come off my dad's voice. It was a tone I'd never heard from him before, not even when I'd come to him as a little girl with a bruise or a cut. "You're right. Mark's not Peter. Did you tell him the one rule?"

My parents had one unbreakable rule with their clients.

They could lie to their families. They could lie to the press. They could lie to the police.

They couldn't lie to my parents because you defended a guilty person differently than you defended an innocent one. My parents didn't want any surprises in court. If they knew the truth, they could prepare for it, whatever it might be.

I hadn't told Mark the rule because I didn't need to.

"I told him," Anderson said.

Of course he would have. He'd modeled so much of his practice on my parents.

"Then we'll get him acquitted." The softness was gone from my dad's voice as quickly as it'd come. "But this'll be one for the wall."

Pain throbbed above my eyes. I rubbed at the spots. *The wall* was a section in my parents' office where they hung news clippings from the most challenging cases they'd won. It was the equivalent of an athlete's trophy shelf.

We didn't talk about the difficult cases that didn't make the wall.

I'd been hoping I was wrong about this case and that my parents would see something obvious that I'd missed.

I planted my feet firmly on the floor and pulled my back up straight. They won more than they lost. They could win this one, too.

I filled them in on what Mark told me about the angry family member and that I already had our private investigator looking into the names.

My parents didn't give out praise, but anytime they didn't criticize, I knew I'd done the right thing.

"What about the evidence?" my mom asked.

I glanced at Anderson. He gave an I'm-not-sure-what-she-means-either head shake.

I inclined my head toward the phone, trying to hint that he should ask.

He made a you-do-it shooing motion with his hands. He might sound professional on the outside, but he still wanted to leave a good impression with my parents, just like a little boy wanting to impress his teacher.

Chicken, I mouthed, then asked, "What do you mean?"

"Who's working on alternate explanations for the cell phone and the scalpel? Mark's innocent." My mom said it in a way that let me know she'd never doubted it the way my dad had. "Their strongest evidence against him is the cell phone and the scalpel with his fingerprints. If we can discredit those, Mark's chances improve dramatically."

The scalpel! Talk about being too close to something to see it clearly. I'd been focused on the *who*, and not enough on the *how*. Someone had to have stolen a scalpel that already had Mark's fingerprints on it. If we could figure out how they'd done it, it might lead us to the real killer.

*T*here was only one place I could think of that someone would have been able to get a scalpel with Mark's fingerprints on it—the morgue.

Because our county was a small one, Mark's office and the morgue were part of Cavanaugh funeral home, run by his brother Grant.

As soon as I was in my car and headed back to Fair Haven, I called Grant's phone. It went straight to voicemail. I left a message. While I could text him, Grant regularly ignored his texts and routinely sent replies to the wrong people. As good as he was with people, he was equally as bad with technology.

I tried his wife, Megan, instead. She answered, and I explained what I needed.

"Come on by." Piano music played faintly in the background. "I'll help when I have a break if you need me, but Grant isn't going to be free for hours. We have a funeral and two visitations going on right now."

I'd always thought it was unfair that life didn't pause for you when something bad happened. Megan and Grant had to keep running their business even though Mark had been accused of murder. I had an advantage. My job allowed me to actively do something about Mark's situation.

I thanked Megan and told her I'd be there in about half an hour. I couldn't stand the idea of going home and not making any more progress today. I'd be so distracted that I shouldn't even be allowed to do anything around Sugarwood anyway.

By the time I got to Cavanaugh Funeral Home, no spaces remained in the parking lot, and cars lined up down the street. I ended up parked two blocks away. Megan hadn't been kidding.

I stopped on the front steps and glanced up. The front of the building had two cameras monitoring it. Having been here at closing a couple of times with Megan, I knew the front door had an alarm keypad and the camera system that turned on as soon as the alarm was armed. It'd seemed excessive to me for a small town. Megan said it was because Mark worked out of the building. The case files and bodies for autopsy had to be kept secure.

The back door would be armed with the same setup.

Megan and Grant hadn't mentioned anything about an attempted break-in. We had to assume the perpetrator knew about the cameras and alarm system. That meant he either had the alarm code and a key to the building, plus knowledge of how to erase the video footage, or he'd gotten in some other way. I didn't know how their video surveillance worked, but if they could tell whether the recordings had been tampered with, we'd be off to a good start. Then we'd unfortunately also have to look at any of their employees who had a key and the code.

Megan stood just inside the front doors, asking people who they were here for and directing them. Her white blouse and black skirt and blazer looked so out of place compared to the colorful clothes she usually wore.

I waited for a slight break in the stream of people and stepped up to her.

She gave me a smile that looked borrowed from someone else. "As soon as the funeral starts, one of our employees is stepping in to give me a quick break. Do you need me for anything?"

I wanted to tell her *no* and that she should use her break to rest, but I did need her help. I explained about the videos.

"I'll check," she said quickly as another group of people flooded through the doors. "We only keep two weeks of footage, but it'll be easy to tell if it was tampered with by running a system report."

I headed down the hall toward the back of the building where Mark's office and the morgue were located. His office would be locked, and not even Megan and Grant had a key, but he didn't keep scalpels in his office anyway.

I swung by the back door and opened it. The key pad flashed, indicating it was still functioning, and the camera looked intact. That meant they hadn't somehow damaged the system to get in unnoticed.

Hopefully Megan found something in the system report.

Halfway down the hall toward where I remembered the morgue to be, Megan caught up with me.

Her face told me the answer before she spoke. "The video wasn't tampered with. Maybe they came more than two weeks ago?"

Maybe. We had to hope that wasn't the case, though. If it was, it'd be a struggle to prove it happened at all.

It was also possible I'd given to much credit to the intruder. The murderer might not have come themselves. They could have bribed or blackmailed one of Grant and Megan's employees to steal a scalpel. That person might not have thought to erase themselves from the video. "Are you able to send the recordings to my firm? I'll have our intern watch through them to see if anyone came in at a time when they shouldn't have."

A long shot perhaps, but it was still a shot.

I texted her the email address for our intern and told Megan what to put in the subject line.

"Excuse me," a soft female voice said from behind Megan. "Could you tell me where the Ainsley visitation is?"

A look of exhaustion flashed over Megan's face. Providing comfort to others when your own heart was troubled had to be one of the most draining things in the world.

She wiped her expression clean before turning around. "You took a left when you should have taken a right. I'll show you."

I continued on in the direction of the morgue. The best thing I could do for Mark and the whole Cavanaugh family was to stay focused and figure this out. They didn't need comfort. Mark wasn't dead. They needed the truth.

I stopped outside the door marked STAFF ONLY. I'd forgotten to ask Meagan for the key, and she'd likely be busy for a while now.

At least I could see if there were any signs of someone clumsily picking the lock. Before I'd learned that there weren't any signs of forced entry into Mark's house, I'd watched over a dozen videos online about lock-picking and read even more articles. The hope was that I'd recognize signs and know which kinds of locks could be picked and how. It turned out I didn't need that information for Mark's house, but it might still come in useful now.

I dropped to one knee so I was eye level with the keyhole, leaned in, and placed a hand on the door to steady myself.

The door swung open, and I planted belly first onto the floor like a seal leaping out of the water and onto dry land.

Oh boy did I hope the floor had been washed recently. Thankfully I'd stopped my fall before my face hit the ground. Even if the floor was perfectly clean, the idea of face-planting onto a morgue floor made my skin want to escape my body.

I crawled back up to my feet. They must leave the door unlocked during the day while they were moving bodies in and out of the mortuary fridge. Regular people would see the STAFF ONLY sign and keep out.

The real killer could have pretended they were here for a visitation or a funeral and have stolen a scalpel. That was good in one way for our argument that it could have been planted.

It was bad in another. I'd hoped we'd be able to narrow down suspects based on who had access to the morgue. Now it seemed like all of Fair Haven could have had access.

Megan should still send the surveillance video to the firm's intern, but the odds were good it wouldn't show anything out of the ordinary.

I needed to go home and raid Nancy's maple syrup candy samples. Everything I tried seemed to arrive at a dead end. Then again, if I did that, I'd need yet another fitting with my wedding dress seamstress because I'd have gained weight.

Either way, it was time to go home. My dogs had been alone all day, and the excited full-body-lean welcome that only big dogs gave would help me almost as much as eating my way into a sugar coma.

What I wasn't willing to do was go back out the front door. Going out the back door would mean a longer walk in the cold, but less chance of running into someone I knew who'd have questions about Mark.

I turned in the direction of the back door.

A woman's voice that I didn't immediately recognize called my name from behind me.

Too late.

I turned slowly. If this was someone who simply wanted gossip, I was going to tell them that I couldn't discuss the case for confidentiality reasons except to say that Mark was innocent.

Mark's house cleaner, Bernice McCloud, huffed down the hallway toward me. Mark and I had been talking just last week about whether to replace Bernice when she retired or to clean our house ourselves.

"I thought that was you," she said. "I'm glad I caught you. I didn't know if I should try to call you or Mark or if he was... Henry told me what happened."

She twisted her fingers together and broke eye contact as if asking if he was in jail would be as bad as suggesting he'd died.

If this was going to be the reaction from people who knew us, I'd found another reason to prove Mark innocent as quickly as possible. I couldn't stand awkward conversations everywhere I went.

Though she might be feeling awkward for an entirely different reason. I knew Bernice and Henry had five boys, two of whom were still in college. One was doing his master's degree. That probably hadn't left them much money. They might live paycheck to paycheck right now. "If you're worried about your check, I'll make sure it's taken care of. It's every other Friday right?"

"It is but..." She pulled at her fingers so hard I worried she might dislocate one. "The thing is I don't...I don't do windows, and I don't do blood."

Oh. Right. Having to ask me about that was even worse than having to remind me about her pay. And I might not have thought of it had she not brought it up. Even though I'd worked with people who'd had crimes happen in their buildings, I'd never been the one to hire the professional crew to clean up the biomatter left behind. Had she not thought of it herself, the poor woman would have gone in to clean Mark's house next week and found a horror scene.

"Take this coming week off—paid of course—and I'll make sure to get someone in to take care of it before the following week, okay?"

She bobbed her head and backed off down the hall, reminding me a bit of a frightened cat who wanted to run from a dog but didn't feel safe turning its back on the other animal.

This day was getting better by the minute—sarcasm most definitely intended. I guess I should look on the bright side. Bernice hadn't outright quit.

One foot from the back door, my phone vibrated in my coat pocket. Maybe Anderson had somehow managed to track down the real owner of the disposable phone. A girl could always hope, despite the logical side of my brain knowing there was no way he could have results that fast.

I grabbed my phone. The name on the screen was Hal's. I slid my finger across the screen to answer.

"This might have been the easiest work you've ever given me, Miss Dawes," Hal said. "But I don't think you're going to like what I've come up with."

For the first time, I wished Hal pulled his punches or sugar-coated things or any of the other clichés that meant he'd soften whatever news I wasn't going to like. "Tell me fast, then."

Fast didn't make ripping a Band-Aid off hurt any less, but it did get the pain over with quicker. Hopefully the same would be true of unpleasant news.

"Westbay teaches school in Washington State now. I found him online first try in a school directory there. The school says he was at work Thursday and Friday, so unless he hired a hitman on a teacher's salary, he's not the guy."

And there went the rest of my hope for a lead on who'd done this. "You're sure you got the right guy."

"His last name's one of the rarest in the U.S., but I called him just in case and pretended I got a piece of his mail, looked important, from the government. Then I read him the address for the guy by the name that lived here in Michigan, and he confirmed it was him."

It'd been a long shot anyway. "What about the other name and license plate number I gave you?"

Please say you found nothing, I silently urged him.

"That one's a weird one. Are you sure you gave me the right name? 'Cause the lady you're looking for doesn't exist."

I drooped back against the wall next to the door. That wasn't the kind of nothing I'd been hoping for.

When I took Isabel's phone number, I'd had her add it and her name directly to my phone. I hadn't wanted to risk not getting it right and missing my opportunity to have fantastic cupcakes at my wedding. "I'm sure the name is correct."

"Well"—I could almost hear him shaking his head on the other end of the call—"I found two Isabel Addingtons. One's eight years old and lives in Colorado, and the other one died in 1940."

13

I shouldn't do what I was considering.

I mimicked Mark's tactic and drove around in circles rather than going straight home, hoping I'd come up with a better idea. Because my only idea right now required me to break into Isabel's food truck to find some evidence of who she really was.

After Hal's announcement that Isabel basically didn't exist, I'd given him her license plate number to run—C6H12O6. I'd remembered it because Mark had laughed so hard he inhaled cupcake into his lungs the first time he saw it. When he finally stopped coughing enough to talk, he'd explained to me why it was so funny. Isabel's license plate number was the chemical equation for glucose.

Hal came back to me with a response almost right away. Her plates were registered to a numbered company incorporated in Florida. He'd run a search for directors to see if he could locate what Isabel's real name might be. He'd come up empty.

The corner to head for Sugarwood came and went, and I turned in the opposite direction again. If I kept this up much longer, I'd need to stop for gas.

Had I known Isabel wasn't who she said she was back when she packaged up the cupcakes yesterday, I could have been careful and taken the package straight to the police. They might have been able to take a print from it.

Though that assumed anyone would have listened to me enough to consider that her prints needed to be run. They wouldn't waste resources on a hunch. It also assumed that her prints would be in the system. Your average person wasn't. If she had no criminal history and no military record, her prints would come back without any potential matches.

Lying to me about her name wasn't a crime. I wasn't federal law enforcement. Being in the same locale as a crime, even while a crime was being committed, wasn't a crime. Unless I could prove Isabel had been directly involved with Troy's death or Chief McTavish's disappearance, I couldn't reliably say she'd done anything wrong.

My one hope was to find something to tell me her real name and then see if Mark recognized her real name or if she had a connection—however slim—to a case he'd worked. He hadn't recognized her, but that didn't mean she wasn't related to someone he'd helped put into prison or someone who hadn't gotten the justice they felt they deserved. She wasn't from this area. The connection might even be from something back before Mark returned to Fair Haven. She might have come here seeking revenge.

That didn't tell me how Troy and Chief McTavish fit into all of this, but finding a link between Isabel and what was happening would get us headed back in a direction where we could prove Mark hadn't been behind it.

My chest suddenly felt full, and my eyes burned. I turned on my hazard lights and pulled over to the side of the road.

I didn't want Isabel to be involved. I liked her.

I'd visited her quite a few times while she created my maple syrup cupcake, and she'd shown me how she came up with new flavors. Even before that, I'd always stood and talked for a few minutes when I bought something from her truck if she wasn't swamped with customers.

One time I'd been there, she'd replaced a cupcake free of charge for a girl who'd dropped the one she bought as she was walking away. Another time she'd helped out a mom who was tight on money but wanted a special cupcake cake for her daughter's thirteenth birthday.

Neither of those things seemed like something a brutal murderer would do.

Then again, I'd been deceived before. Isabel also didn't smile nearly as much as someone who worked around sweets should. That could point toward something in her past that still haunted her—something for which she wanted vengeance.

I put my car back into drive and headed for Sugarwood.

I had to find out Isabel's real name, either to clear her or to find a link between her and the three men. She might be using a different name for some other reason. Hopefully not one that would require me to reveal her real identity to the police—like that she had a warrant out for her arrest in another state.

And if I was doing this—if I was really going to break into

Isabel's truck—I had to do it on my own. Even though I wasn't going to take anything other than pictures, breaking into her truck was trespassing at best. Anyone who spotted me could assume I meant to steal her truck. I wasn't going to put someone I cared about into that position if we were seen. Besides, I couldn't think of anyone who wouldn't try to talk me out of this except Elise, and the stakes were too high for her if she got caught breaking into someone's vehicle.

It shouldn't be dangerous, at least. If I waited until midnight, her truck would be empty. She'd have gone home for the night, and I'd have plenty of time before she came back to start the truck for the next day.

All my hours spent studying lock picking on the Internet should even let me get in without damaging her truck. I wouldn't have the skills to jimmy the actual driver's or passenger's door, but the door on the back of the truck that she'd let me in the other day had an old handle—she'd said so herself when she'd been worried about the draft.

All I needed to know was where she'd parked. Isabel had a tendency to leave her truck where she planned to run it from the next day rather than taking it back to wherever she stayed.

But I knew how to find out where it would be.

I waited until I stopped my car in front of my house and pulled out my phone.

I'd like to meet first thing Monday morning to talk flavors, I texted her. *Where can I find you?*

ON SUNDAY NIGHT, WHEN I PULLED INTO THE GRAVEL PARKING lot, Isabel's truck hunched in the darkness right where she'd said it'd be.

This location was one of the most isolated she'd chosen yet. It was one of the small lakeside lots that could only accommodate a couple of cars. Two or three picnic tables—I couldn't tell exactly how many in the shadows cast by the trees—rested in a clearing to the right. In the summer, it'd be a beautiful picnic spot overlooking the lake.

I turned off my car, hit the button that turned off my dome lights so the interior lights wouldn't come back on when I opened the door, and waited to make sure no one had spotted me pulling in. If an officer on patrol had seen me make the turn or saw my lights when I exited, they might follow me to check. They could think my car belonged to kids who'd come here to do things they shouldn't or someone who was lost or having car trouble.

I'd have an awfully hard time explaining my presence if they came to check and found me picking the lock on Isabel's truck.

The cold crept into my feet first, making my toes ache, and then into my hands, straight through the gloves I'd chosen. I'd selected them because they were thin and I hadn't wanted bulky gloves impeding my ability to jimmy the lock. Major miscalculation. If I got much colder, my fingers would either be too numb or shaking too hard to manage the lock.

I climbed out and scurried over to the door that went into the body of the truck. Waiting in my car had given me one benefit. My eyes had adjusted better to the dark than they would have if I'd gotten out immediately.

The lock was exactly the type I'd remembered. Isabel should look into having it upgraded. Any amateur who wanted to rob her could easily pop the lock if I'd figured out how from studying online.

Of course, knowing how to do it and being able to do it were two entirely different things.

I worked at the lock for long enough that my nose started to run and my lips felt dry and ready to crack. I stopped long enough to blow my nose.

One more try and I'd have to give up.

The lock popped open. Thank goodness. At least I'd be able to get out of the wind, and once I was inside, I'd use my cell phone light to search.

I tugged the door open and hopped up the stairs. I drew the door closed behind me, shutting out most of the moonlight and blinding me in darkness until my eyes adjusted.

And I wasn't cold anymore.

The inside of the truck was much too warm.

A cold line of metal that had to be a knife pressed against my neck in the same spot where Troy had his throat slit.

"I was hoping I was wrong about you," Isabel's voice said out of the darkness. "How much do you know?"

a searing pain formed in my chest where my collarbones met, and my own heartbeat filled my ears.

I'd been an idiot. I missed the signs. The way Isabel always had me come to her truck. The way she always parked her truck in isolated locations. The little camping heater she always seemed to have set up.

Isabel—or whatever her name really was—lived in her truck. It wouldn't have mattered when I tried to break in. She would have caught me no matter what.

And now I was very likely going to die, my neck slit just like Troy's. Because there was no other reason for her to be holding a knife to my neck than that she played a role in what happened and she knew I'd figured it out. Most people would call the police if they thought someone was attempting to break into their home or vehicle. They wouldn't lie in wait to ambush them.

At least if I vanished tonight, Mark couldn't be blamed for it.

He was still in a cell at the Fair Haven police station, and he wouldn't be released until tomorrow.

Focus, Nicole. You're panicking again.

I had to stall. I had to stall until my eyes adjusted. Then she'd have one less advantage, and maybe I could still figure a way out of this.

She'd asked me a question. What had she asked me? Something about what I knew? "Know about what?"

Great. That sounded bright and not at *all* fake. But I needed to get her talking, and I wasn't about to tell her what little I'd figured out about this case. Given I was here, she probably wouldn't believe me if I did anyway. It must look like I knew a lot more than I did.

"I don't want to hurt you, okay? I just need to know how much you've told him."

Told Mark? Or did she mean Anderson? There couldn't be another *him* who mattered in this case.

The knife stayed perfectly still on my neck, which was a bit odd. I'd have expected her to add to the threat by increasing the pressure.

My heartbeat slowed enough that I could hear other sounds. Like Isabel's ragged breathing, almost like she was afraid.

It didn't make sense for her to be afraid, though. I was a lot less threatening than the men she'd already faced and bested, and what I knew wouldn't matter once she killed me. Maybe she was afraid that killing me wouldn't be the end of it. That must be it. She wanted to know how much I'd told Anderson so she knew whether she could get away with killing only me or if she'd have to go after him next as well.

Unfortunately, the only good response was the truth. I'd brought this on myself by stupidly coming here alone. Anderson didn't deserve to die because I'd let my desperation to save Mark cloud my normally sound judgment—though in my defense, I had expected her to be sleeping somewhere else. What kind of a crazy person slept in their vehicle during a record-cold Michigan winter anyway?

The fact that her housing choices entered my mind at all let me know I needed to pull my mind back on track again because it was trying hard to slide into the panic circle.

"I haven't told him anything," I said.

"I haven't stayed alive this long by being stupid. He'd demand results, which means you've had to give him something."

The knife blade broke contact with my skin and interior lights flared on. My eyes instinctively squinted at the change. The knife landed back on my neck.

My mind felt like it split, with half still focused on the blade at my throat and the other half working to make sense of Isabel's words.

Anderson wasn't my boss. He couldn't demand results from me. In fact, in this case he was almost working for me, since Mark was my fiancé. Isabel might not realize all of that, though. I couldn't remember exactly, but I didn't think I'd explained my strange job situation to her. It'd make sense to assume that since I also worked at Sugarwood, I wasn't a full partner in Anderson's firm, but rather an employee who'd have to justify her time spent by producing results.

The only thing I could think to do was tell her that and pray she'd believe me. I didn't even have a way to warn Anderson that danger was headed his way. "We're partners. I don't have to report to him."

The corners of Isabel's eyes tightened, and a tiny line appeared between her eyebrows. "He doesn't have partners. He has people he can control."

She rolled her lips together in a way that made me think she was trying not to cry.

"Please." She pulled the knife back slightly. "Just tell me if he knows this name and about my truck, and I'll let you go."

Wait, what? *This* name, not her real name? She should expect Anderson would know the alias she was using. And Anderson wasn't some sort of domineering man. Even my dad partnered with my mom, and my dad was his role model.

Something about this conversation wasn't right. "I don't think we're talking about the same thing. Who are you talking about?"

The tip of the knife wobbled, as if she couldn't decide whether to raise it back up to my neck or set it down permanently. "My husband."

Her tone carried enough hesitation to let me know that she still wasn't convinced whether I was playing her or not.

If Isabel took on an alias to hide from her husband, then she might be innocent of everything I'd been investigating. That meant the knife in her hand was more like a dog who was showing its teeth and growling out of fear.

I had to show her I wasn't a threat. "As far as I know, I've never met your husband. He didn't send me to find you."

"Then why are you here?"

My face suddenly felt like I'd leaned too close to a fire. I was going to sound awfully stupid telling a woman trying to hide from her husband that I thought her guilty of murdering one police officer and kidnapping another.

All her actions made sense in light of a potentially abusive husband chasing her. The fake name. No permanent address. Even how she made sure to lock the door. It probably had nothing to do with the old lock and everything to do with her fear that he'd catch her and she wouldn't see him coming.

But I had the feeling she'd know if I was lying to her about my real reason for coming. That would lead her to assume I was lying about not knowing her husband. I'd have to admit to the truth, embarrassing or not.

"Your behavior was suspicious, and I thought you might be involved with the case involving my fiancé." I spit the words out quickly and quietly. "I was trying to find out your real name so that I could see if you were connected to any of the cases he'd worked."

Isabel laid the knife down on the counter behind her, but she placed it well out of my reach, as if to say *I'm willing to believe you, but I'm not willing to take any chances, just in case.*

I could accept that. I would have done the same thing, and all I really cared about was that there wasn't a knife pointed at me anymore.

She clutched the edge of the counter with one hand. "I wasn't involved in killing anyone or kidnapping anyone."

The way she said it and her specific choice of wording set off my the-witness-is-withholding-information warning signals again, but I was starting to think that was simply Isabel's way. From what I knew of abusive relationships, the victim usually learned early on to hold in their thoughts and emotions, especially if any of them might set off their abuser. That tendency wasn't something Isabel would be able to shut off around other people if it was a skill she'd worked hard on for years.

We continued to stare at each other. Any other time, staring into the eyes of another woman standing this close to me would have felt weird and intrusive. Right now, it was more like neither of us trusted the other quite enough to look away.

"How can I be sure you're telling the truth?" she finally asked. "If I let you leave here, and you're lying to me, he'll know about my truck, and he'll eventually find me. He'll kill me when that happens."

I heard what she didn't say. That if I was lying to her, I'd be a party to murder. It was smart of her not to state it explicitly. Had I been lying, the implication would have had more impact than a blunt statement ever could have.

Thankfully, I was telling the truth.

Now I needed to convince her of it. Not only because I didn't want her to be afraid and have to flee, but also because she was much too talented a baker to give up her truck. If her husband knew about her cupcake truck, she wouldn't just need to change her name or change the name of her business. She'd have to abandon it entirely and start over in a new career, probably one completely outside of the food industry. She couldn't risk leaving any trail for him to follow if she wanted to survive.

"I'm a criminal lawyer, not a private investigator. I only represent clients who are innocent. My fiancé is the county medical examiner, and two of my closest friends here are police officers. I try to work with the good guys."

Isabel rubbed her hand along her neck like she was having trouble swallowing or breathing. Maybe both. "The good guys."

The way she echoed my words made me feel like I was missing something again.

She tried to step backward and bumped into the counter. "Your association with the police is one of the reasons I was afraid you were helping my husband. The police aren't always the good guys."

The sadness in her voice made my throat ache.

Her husband couldn't be...but there wasn't any other option that made sense. Her husband was either a law enforcement officer or he worked with them.

I wanted to defend the police. Most police officers were the good guys. Most of them wanted to protect the innocent and serve their community. They were willing to put their own lives in danger to do so. They worked long hours and faced a lot of stress and situations that would break the average person.

But even I couldn't argue they were all good. Look at former Chief Wilson and Chief McTavish's ongoing corruption investigation.

Oh no. My vision went fuzzy, and I felt a bit like I might throw up.

How could I have missed it? There was one other case, if you could call it that, that Mark, Troy, and Chief McTavish might have had in common—the ongoing investigation into corruption within the Fair Haven PD.

I forced myself to take a few deep breaths, and my vision slowly cleared. Isabel gave me a look that said she didn't know whether to get me a paper bag to breathe in to or tie me up and drop me somewhere so she could make her escape.

"You're right," I said. "Not all police are the good guys, and I think I just figured out why an officer I knew was murdered and my fiancé was framed for it."

15

"Sit down over there"—Isabel pointed at a thick pile of blankets that had to be her bed—"before you fall over."

I obeyed because at least she wasn't pointing a knife at me anymore, and it wasn't like I could do anything about what I'd figured out, considering it was the middle of the night. "Does this mean you believe me that your husband didn't send me?"

"It means that if you crack your head on my counter, I'll have to call 911, and there'll be no way my husband won't find me then." I thought I caught a hint of a smile.

Isabel put a pot onto a burner, spooned in sugar and cocoa powder, and added milk.

I'd broken into her truck in the middle of the night, thinking she was a murderer, and she was making me homemade cocoa. She was either the nicest person I'd ever met or she'd spent so much time trying to soothe an abuser that she couldn't break the caregiver habit. It might be a bit of both.

Truth was, I didn't care why she was doing it. It felt like what I imagined it would have been like if I had an older sister. I would have sneaked into her room late at night and talked through my problems with her in the way that I never could with my parents.

She handed me a mug and settled in next to me. She tented her knees up and rested her mug on top in a way that said she expected to have me tell her what was going on.

I explained my theory. "Now I don't know what to do. Normally, if I thought I'd found something relating to the corruption investigation, I'd take it to Chief McTavish."

Isabel wrapped her hands around her mug. Given the warmth in the truck, it couldn't be because her fingers were cold. Whatever she planned to say must make her uncomfortable.

"You can't go to the police," she said. "Whoever's behind this made sure of that."

My first reaction was to say that was her natural distrust of the police talking, but she was right. By implicating Mark in Troy's murder and making Chief McTavish vanish, they'd ensured I didn't have an official channel to turn to. It was brilliant, really. They'd cast blame and protected themselves all at the same time.

The only people left in the Fair Haven police department were strangers who wouldn't believe me because they thought I might have aided and abetted Mark, and officers we couldn't trust because they might be part of the web of corruption.

I took a long, slow sip of the hot cocoa. It coated my tongue in chocolate sweetness in a way that hot chocolate from a package couldn't, and the warmth spread far beyond my stomach. It might feel a bit hopeless right now, but I wasn't completely alone. "I guess the place to start is to figure out if there's anyone we can trust."

Isabel glanced at me sidelong. "That's always the place to start."

I'd have told her she could trust me if I thought it'd make any difference, but I got the impression that she placed more weight on actions than on words.

"Is there anyone other than your missing chief who would know who he'd already cleared and who he suspected?" Isabel asked.

Mark might, but it wasn't likely. He'd told me Chief McTavish wanted to keep him in the dark about his conclusions so that Mark could approach the files and old autopsies McTavish handed him without bias. I knew McTavish—at least early on—hadn't confided in Erik. Because Erik was second-in-command after former Chief Wilson, he'd been one of the primary suspects initially.

I shook my head.

Isabel swirled her mug around like she was thinking, but it could simply be that she was trying to mix any sugar and cocoa powder that'd separated from the milk back together. My brain was still working overtime trying to figure her out.

"I wish there was something more I could do to help." Her voice had a tone that begged me to understand everything she wanted to say but couldn't. "But I can't be around the police."

"It's okay. It's not like you could find out something I couldn't anyway."

She opened her mouth, closed it again, and got to her feet.

She drained her cup and placed it in the sink. "Are you feeling steady enough to drive now?"

I had to be. I couldn't continue to camp out on the floor of Isabel's food truck all night. I should get some sleep. Mark would be out on bail tomorrow. He could write down all the cases he remembered that he'd flagged as suspicious for Chief McTavish. Maybe if we pooled our brains with Elise, Erik, and Anderson, we could spot a link between them.

It was a long shot. If it were an obvious link, Chief McTavish would have closed the case long ago. But it was what we could do, and Elise and Mark had the advantage of having grown up in Fair Haven. That alone might provide them with the missing link when they looked at it all together.

I handed my mug up to Isabel and got to my feet, trying not to step on her bed.

I glanced down at the rumpled bedding. I had enough troubles of my own to worry about, but I couldn't simply walk away and leave her here. "I have big dogs."

Isabel gave me a look that said that before she'd had it beaten out of her—by life, her husband, or both—she'd had a strong sense of humor and the ability to see the absurdity around her and laugh. "Good for you."

That wasn't quite the clear invitation I'd intended it to be. In my defense, I wasn't a night owl. My normal bedtime was hours ago. "What I mean is that you'd be safer staying with me than staying here. My dogs are a great early warning system."

"I don't really sleep anyway. I heard your car as soon as you pulled up, and I was already watching you before you ever stepped out." Isabel slowly rinsed out her mug, then mine, and set them upside down on a dish cloth to dry. "Besides, I can't put you in that kind of danger. My husband…"

Her gaze shifted to the side, and for an irrational second, I thought she spotted him out the window. She might get more sleep staying with me, but it seemed like I might not. That didn't mean I was going to retract my offer, though. I couldn't leave her living in her truck when I had a perfectly good guest room.

Her gaze came back to my face and she licked her lips. "Was Chief McTavish married?"

I nodded.

"My husband would sometimes tell me things he probably shouldn't have. Chief McTavish might have said something about the corruption investigation to his wife."

THE NEXT MORNING, ON MY DRIVE TO THE MCTAVISH HOME, MY yawns were so large they could be considered distracted driving.

I'd been right about getting less sleep than Isabel if she came to my house. It'd taken me another fifteen minutes of convincing after her suggestion that I talk to Mrs. McTavish, but I'd finally won out when I told her we could park her truck back in my sugar bush. Even if her husband somehow knew about her truck, he'd never see it there, and most cupcake decorators didn't live with their clients. My house was probably the last place he'd think to look.

She'd still been sleeping when I left. It might be the first good night's sleep she'd had in months—or longer, depending on when she escaped her husband.

Erik had texted me Chief McTavish's address this morning. He hadn't asked why I wanted it. The paranoid part of me wondered if he wanted plausible deniability in case one of the detectives investigating McTavish's disappearance asked him why I'd want to visit. The truth was probably closer to that he was distracted and hadn't thought it through far enough to wonder about it.

My GPS took me to what I'd consider a middle-class section of Fair Haven. It was off the lakeshore, but they were single-family homes with yards.

I parked in the driveway and headed for the door. Before I could reach it, Mrs. McTavish came out, dressed in a woolen winter coat and gloves, her purse over her shoulder. No scarf or hat meant she'd likely been born a northerner. Most days when I went out, you could barely see my face with the way I bundled up.

She stopped with one hand on the door knob and a cautious expression that probably came from being a long-time cop's wife. "May I help you?"

"I'm Nicole Fitzhenry-Dawes."

All Isabel's talk about not being able to trust the police must be getting to me because an explanation of why I was here stuck in my throat like it was afraid someone might overhear me.

Mrs. McTavish's gaze swept her street almost as if she also expected someone to be watching us. "You're investigating?"

Chief McTavish had clearly said something about me to his wife. I nodded.

She held open the door, and I stepped inside. Up close, her

eyes and nose had the extra-pink appearance of someone who'd been crying.

The center of my chest twisted. At least I knew where Mark was. I might not like where he was, but I didn't have to lie awake at night wondering if he was alive or not.

Mrs. McTavish hung up her coat and slid off her shoes, another sign that she was born somewhere north of the Mason-Dixon Line. It was strange that I knew so little about her. We'd only met a couple of times at department events where family was invited. As far as I knew, she didn't socialize much at all.

I left my coat and shoes by the door as well. I'd been here long enough now that I'd known to wear respectable socks instead of the ones I had with monkeys or kittens on them when I was going to someone else's house.

She motioned me to a chair but didn't offer me anything to drink, almost as if she didn't want any delays. "What can I do to help?"

My conscience wouldn't let me stretch the truth to her about my role. She should know up front. "My investigation isn't official."

"I never thought it was." She had a sharp way of speaking, almost as if she'd been military or law enforcement herself at some point. Or maybe that just came from years of living around them. "Owen said you're always sticking your nose in where it doesn't belong."

Ouch.

"He also said you're one of the best he's ever met. He probably didn't tell you this, but he tried to get permission to hire you as a consultant on the case he was sent here for."

He hadn't told me that. I wish it'd been approved. I'd be much further ahead now. Or I'd be dead.

Maybe not being involved up until this point was a blessing in disguise.

I caught her up on the little I did know and why I'd come.

"Owen couldn't say much, obviously, but he would tell me when he cleared someone. He knew how hard I found it to see the people he worked with and wonder which ones I shouldn't turn my back on." She reached a hand out to the end table beside her and felt around. "Let me grab a pen and paper."

It seemed there were a lot of things I hadn't known and hadn't even considered about Chief McTavish—like the effect his job would have on his wife. How could you make friends in a new place when you didn't know who your husband might uncover as a criminal? What McTavish did was different from simple police work. His wife couldn't even trust his coworkers because he was only sent to places where corruption was suspected.

She went around the back of her chair and opened a door almost directly behind it. She left it hanging open and disappeared inside. Brown packing boxes lined the far wall, some open but most taped shut.

The skin on the back of my neck did a little shudder-shiver.

Chief McTavish had been here for nearly a year now. There shouldn't still be boxes from when they'd moved in. And as far as I knew, he hadn't been close enough to unraveling the corruption situation to be packing to leave already.

So why did his wife look like she was stowing their life up in boxes only days after her husband went missing?

She came back out with the paper and pen and shut the door behind her. She sat back in her chair and jotted names down on the list.

"Were you two thinking of moving to a new place?" I said as casually as I could manage. "I noticed your boxes."

Her pen stopped, and she looked up.

"Owen was right about you." Tiny lines showed at the corner of her eyes, but I couldn't tell if they were because she wanted to narrow her eyes at me or because she was laughing at me inside. "I'm not planning to skip town, if that's what you're thinking."

Her tone didn't carry censure or guilt, so my guess was she found it funny that I suspected her. I wasn't going to let that distract me from the question, though. It was still one that felt like it needed an answer. I'd seen too many people dodge questions by laughing off the possible motives behind them. "Then why the boxes?"

The laugh lines disappeared, and her pen drooped. "I stopped unpacking completely a long time ago. We rarely stay anywhere long enough for it to feel worthwhile. Why take out my gardening gear if we'll be somewhere else before spring, or why unpack the extra sets of sheets if our kids won't be able to get vacation time to visit before we leave again?"

If we managed to find Chief McTavish and he was alright, he was probably going to hate that I'd gotten this look into his private life. In my defense, I wouldn't have pried had I not worried his wife might be hiding something.

Mrs. McTavish had turned her attention back to her paper and was writing again. "His job was the one thing we truly argued about. I wanted him to quit internal investigations years ago." She glanced up. "It wasn't just the moves, either. It always took a toll on him, knowing no one had his back at work, and they wished he wasn't there."

It reminded me a bit of how I'd felt before I came to Fair Haven. I'd had few true friends, and I'd always felt like the people I worked with were nice to me because I was the bosses' daughter. It wasn't until I came to Fair Haven that I started to feel I'd found a place to belong. "There are people who'd like to see him stay here. I'm one of them."

She gave me a smile that was sad around the edges. "I know. He'd finally agreed that this would be his last Internal Affairs job, and he'd applied to keep the job as Fair Haven chief of police. Sergeant Higgins wanted to plan a surprise party when it became official, after this corruption investigation was closed. This one's been the worst yet. Every lead turns out to be another rabbit trail laid down to veer him off course." She folded the paper up and handed it to me. "Now it might all be too late."

I wanted to make her all sorts of promises, but I knew better. Chief McTavish was a good officer. Mark was a good medical examiner. They'd been struggling at this for months. There were no guarantees I'd figure this out, and there were even fewer that I'd figure it out in time to save Chief McTavish, wherever he was.

Instead of saying anything, I accepted the paper and slipped it into my purse.

She walked me to the door and pulled my coat from the rack.

"I know you think you're always careful when you're investigating a case, but don't take even the smallest risk this time." She extended my coat to me, but didn't release it when I took hold.

"Owen told me one more thing about this case. The former chief wasn't the puppet master. He was an underling brought in to expand the operation. Whoever is behind all of this is still walking free. We don't know who he is, but I'm sure he knows that you'll eventually make the connection and start hunting for him. That means he might already be planning to hunt you first."

16

I was thankful Anderson was handling Mark's bail hearing because Mrs. McTavish's warning didn't leave much room in my head for anything else.

I'd assumed Chief Wilson was the one who came up with the corruption scheme in Fair Haven. He'd wanted a perfect record so that he could make a run for county sheriff. A little extra money to pad his lifestyle hadn't hurt, either.

It'd never crossed my mind that Wilson could have been recruited by someone else.

Isabel was gone by the time I got home. She'd left me a note about making deliveries and that she would be back later. That was probably for the best. I'd already shared too much about this case with her.

It also left me with time to kill until Mark was released and we could figure out what to do next.

I took the dogs for a quick walk in the bush, making sure to dress them in their special I'm-not-a-deer jackets even though hunting season was over. Russ had tried to assure me that no one was allowed to hunt on Sugarwood property anyway, so we'd have been safe, but I wasn't taking chances. As soon as I found out about hunting season, I'd gotten Mandy to help me create a big orange jacket that I could Velcro over top of the jackets I put on them to keep them warm.

They looked a bit like traffic cones with legs afterwards, but no one could claim they'd mistaken them for a deer.

The dogs settled in for their post-walk nap as soon as we got home, leaving me alone with the slip of paper Mrs. McTavish had given me.

I swear it'd gotten heavier the longer I carried it without looking at it. It was childish to continue to wait simply because I was afraid of whose name might not be on the list.

I took it from my purse and smoothed it out, but didn't look at it immediately.

I couldn't be a baby about it now. We had to know where to start. It was my whole reason for going to see Mrs. McTavish.

Just because someone's name wasn't on here didn't mean they were involved with what had happened. It only meant Chief McTavish hadn't been able to fully clear them yet. They could still be innocent.

I forced my gaze down to the list. It was longer than I'd expected. The first step would be to see who was missing.

I pulled out a fresh piece of paper. I'd write down everyone before reading the list carefully to avoid missing anyone out of some subconscious bias.

The Fair Haven police department had twenty-two employees, including Chief McTavish. Only sixteen of those were police officers. Mark, the three dispatchers, the chaplain, and the part-time counsellor weren't sworn officers of the law. Mark, the chaplain, and the counsellor weren't even directly tied to the Fair Haven PD. They served the whole county.

I numbered twenty-one spaces and started writing names. Thankfully I'd always had a good memory, and I'd been around the police department long enough now that I'd dealt with almost everyone.

I filled the list and then started crossing names off of mine.

Elise and Erik had both been cleared. I knew they would have, but it felt good to have my faith in them confirmed.

So had Troy.

Seeing his name on Mrs. McTavish's list loosened something in my chest. I hadn't realized it, but I must have been afraid Troy had been part of the corruption scheme and had been betrayed by his partner or partners. I'd rather think of him as a good man who died trying to do what was right.

Mrs. McTavish hadn't written down any of the adjunct names, including Mark's. Chief McTavish had cleared Mark first. That meant those names weren't absent because they hadn't been cleared. With that many absent names sharing the one thing in common, it seemed like Chief McTavish had been focused on the police officers.

I didn't have enough background to know if that was because he knew something about the corruption situation that meant it could only have been an officer running it all or if he simply considered them less likely and was leaving them for last. Though that seemed backwards to how I would have operated. Most people would cross off the easiest suspects first.

I put a single X through the block of names and went back to matching up officers.

Only three officers' names were missing when I finished.

Brandon Rigman, Grady Scherwin, and Quincey Dornbush.

"IT'S NOT QUINCEY," MARK SAID WHEN I SHOWED HIM THE LIST later that afternoon. "I know Quincey."

I'd crossed Quincey's name off, written it back on, rinse and repeat so many times while waiting for Mark that I'd had to get a new piece of paper. I nudged the paper closer to Mark across my kitchen counter. "Was there anything in the autopsy reports that Chief McTavish had you review that could link to Quincey?"

Mark shook his head. "But I can say the same about Rigman and Scherwin. Scherwin didn't work any of the cases."

Which meant there was still something Chief McTavish knew that we didn't. "Maybe he did clear Quincey, but he hadn't had a chance to tell his wife yet."

"Maybe." Mark glanced down at his lap and shifted a hand. One of the dogs must have read into his tone of voice and decided he needed some comfort. "The best thing we can do is figure out the leader behind all this. That won't directly clear Quincey, but it'll be a step."

Mark didn't have to say it would also help clear him. It spoke loudly to the kind of man he was that, instead of going to Elise and Erik's house to rest and clean up, he'd come straight here to work the case. His personal effects still sat in a plastic bag on my kitchen counter.

I flipped the list of names over. We'd both remember them, and we didn't need Quincey's name staring us in the face, distracting us. "Whoever's in charge of this had already started before former Chief Wilson joined. Mrs. McTavish made it sound like the ringleader helped Wilson become chief."

We had to assume the ringleader didn't approach anyone and everyone, trying to recruit them. He must see something in them that made him think he could convince them to look the other way when he told them to. Wilson had certainly been ambitious enough.

That was another tick in favor of Quincey not being involved. He wasn't at all ambitious. He was happy to live a quiet life in Fair Haven, and he hadn't even tried for a promotion.

Rigman had plans to move into crime scene reconstruction. That was a goal, but it didn't match as cleanly as Wilson's goals for advancement would have.

Grady Scherwin, though, liked power and prestige. I didn't believe in reincarnation, but if I did, Grady Scherwin would come back as a peacock one day.

"Do you know how Chief Wilson became chief?" I asked.

Mark's hand continued to stroke whoever sat by his knee. It had to be Toby. Velma was the more affectionate one normally, but she also stayed still about as well as a fly at a picnic. I'd been told by the few other Great Dane owners that I'd met that Velma would settle down once she turned two. That seemed like a life-time away.

"I was still in New York when he took over," Mark said, "but the previous chief—John Zacharius—had an accident."

The way Mark said *accident*, with a gravity reserved only for delivering bad news, I knew the accident had been fatal.

"Wilson became the interim chief, and you know the rest."

The rest was that Fair Haven's crime rate appeared to go down under Chief Wilson's leadership. What no one had known at the time was that was because he'd chosen to cover up a lot of what was actually happening, presumably not only to set himself up for sheriff one day but also because he was receiving a lucrative payoff.

Mark stilled. A whine issued from near him, but he was on his feet. "I have the file. Chief McTavish passed it along to me a day or two before Troy died. I hadn't had a chance to go through it in detail yet."

If he had the case file for Chief Zacharius' seemingly accidental death, then we were definitely on the right path. McTavish must have come to the same conclusion we had.

We had to get that file. "Where is it?"

"At my house."

We tucked the dogs into their crates and headed for Mark's house. I let him drive. I'd have been too tempted to speed.

He parked in his driveway. With the crime scene tape gone, I wouldn't have known that anything bad had happened here only a few days ago. His house looked like it always had.

I reached for the door handle.

Mark laid a hand on my arm, stopping me. "The clean-up crew won't be here until tomorrow, right?"

"That was the soonest they had an opening."

"You'd better stay here. The smell will be one you won't be able to forget."

I shuddered, removed my fingers from the door handle, and gave Mark's hand a quick squeeze.

"I won't be gone long," he said, and then he was out of the car and headed for the house.

A minute ticked by. Then two.

My ribs started to ache like my lungs were trying to push their way out. I sucked in a breath and realized I hadn't been breathing. It shouldn't be taking Mark this long to find the file. His office at Cavanaugh Funeral Home was one of the neatest I'd ever seen, and that was saying something, given that I'd worked for my parents and they didn't tolerate messiness in their firm.

Could the murderer have come back now that the scene was released? They couldn't plant any more evidence against Mark, but they could plan to attack him and stage a suicide. That would instantly close the case. The detectives investigating were so sure Mark was guilty that they wouldn't question whether his suicide was real or not.

Mark came out the door, and I slumped back in my seat. The sooner this case was solved, the better. I was heading straight for a stress ulcer at this point.

He slid back into the car, but his hands were empty—something I'd missed in my relief that the murderer wasn't forcing pills down his throat or stringing him up.

"It wasn't there?"

Mark shook his head. "I don't understand it. It shouldn't have been confiscated as evidence. It'd be clear to anyone who looked that it had nothing to do with Troy or me. Neither of us were even in Fair Haven at the time. And no one should have taken it thinking it was an open case. All the open cases are kept in my office at the funeral home where it's more secure, and this file was clearly marked CLOSED."

The police weren't the only ones in his home lately. If we were right about the connection this *accidental* death had to the corruption scheme in Fair Haven, then there was someone else with a strong motive to take it. "Could the murderer have stolen it when he killed Troy?"

That would help explain why he'd chosen to kill Troy in Mark's home. He'd had two things he needed to do—frame Mark and make sure that file vanished.

"The file I had was just a copy." Mark massaged the spot above his right eye, the spot that meant he was getting a headache. "Taking it wouldn't have stopped someone else from looking at it."

"No, but would anyone else have been looking for it? You and Chief McTavish were the only ones working on the corruption case."

He kept his fingers pressed into the spot above his eye. It made him look a bit like he was trying to hold himself together the old-fashioned way. "As far as I know, yes. The timing is more coincidental than I'm comfortable with."

If we were right, then Chief McTavish reinvestigating the death of the previous chief could have been the trigger that set all of this in motion. The ringleader knew that file could point straight back to him somehow. He had to stop both Mark and Chief McTavish from examining it closely and telling anyone about what they found.

Killing them both would have immediately drawn suspicion. Instead, he'd made Chief McTavish disappear, and he'd done what he could to make sure Mark wouldn't be working any cases ever again.

"With McTavish gone," Mark was saying, "it could be months before they replace him, and whoever they send would have to try to catch up on what he'd already done. They might never make the same connections."

At the very least, it would delay things long enough for the ringleader to cover all his tracks and slip away.

The idea that he'd slink away like that grated on my mind a bit, like it didn't fit with how meticulous and determined he'd shown himself to be. It seemed like he was much more inclined to find a way to keep and expand what he'd put in place than to give it up and flee. He liked the situation he'd created for himself, and he'd spent years cultivating it.

Maybe he felt that this time he had no choice.

If we were going to prove who was behind all of this, we needed that file. And the only place to get a copy was the Fair Haven police station.

17

*M*ark put the car into drive. "Let's make sure the police didn't take the file before we do anything rash."

Mrs. McTavish's warning still burned in my ears every time there was a moment of silence. This was a good time to be methodical rather than rash. We didn't need to be drawing the killer's attention by poking around if it wasn't going to help us identify him. "How do you plan to do that?"

"Ask."

At first, I thought he meant he wanted me to ask him again. Then it clicked that he planned to simply ask the police if they took the file from his house. While we'd eventually have access to a list of the evidence they'd taken from his house that the prosecution planned to use in their case against him, that list wouldn't include an unrelated file that'd been taken because it was police property.

"Detective Dillion isn't going to tell you that. He thinks you killed someone."

Mark gave me a *trust me* smile that made his dimples pop out. "I'm going to tell him that I have to be sure everything is accounted for when my temporary replacement takes over. If they didn't collect that file already, I want to be sure to take it to my office and leave it with whoever is filling in."

Sneaky. And brilliant. And much too much like something I would have come up with. "I think I'm a bad influence on you."

"Let's wait to see whether I succeed or not before we call it good or bad."

He parallel parked in front of the police station like parallel parking was easy and he wasn't about to try to get evidence that could clear his name from the very man who thought he was guilty. He should have been a surgeon on live people instead of dead ones. I bet his hands never shook.

"If we're really lucky," I said, "he'll have it and he'll let you take it with you now to bring to your replacement."

His smile didn't quite make it deep enough to create dimples this time though. "Keep the getaway car warm."

FOR THE SECOND TIME TODAY, MARK CAME BACK TO THE CAR with empty hands.

He had the same look to him as someone who hadn't eaten in twenty-four hours, kind of pale and shaky. He didn't have to tell me what had happened. The police hadn't taken the file. Whoever killed Troy had.

I still needed to hear it. "I guess we still need the file."

"We still need the file." Mark scrubbed his hands over the steering wheel like he didn't know what to do with them otherwise. "We can't walk into a station full of detectives who think I'm a murderer and nab the file."

I held in a snort at his use of the word *nab*, like we were playing cops and robbers. It was the kind of word Elise would think was perfectly normal to use.

The fact that I still found it humorous given the circumstances showed how much I was feeling the stress. I'd be crazy-laughing soon if we weren't careful.

He was right despite his odd word choice. Not only was trying to get a file from the police station ourselves impractical, but it came a bit too close to theft. Mark still technically had a right to that file. He'd been assigned it by Chief McTavish, and it dealt with an independent case. Detective Dillion wouldn't see it that way, though.

On the upside, if he caught us trying to take the file, he might at least look at it and investigate why we wanted it so badly.

Then he'd throw us both in jail for tampering with an active investigation.

"We need someone else to get us a copy of the file," I said before I'd thought it through.

Mark put the car in drive and pulled out onto the road. If I hadn't known him as well, I might have thought he was planning to take us to someone who could help. I did know him. We'd be driving in circles as soon as he could get out onto the main roads. It was his version of pacing. Hopefully it worked better for him that it had for me. I'd driven around for nearly an hour, and I still ended up breaking into Isabel's food truck.

"Who?" Mark asked. "Everyone who's been taken off active duty has also had their access restricted. They can't get to the files any more than we can. They're not even supposed to go to the station."

We passed by the police station. I almost wished Mark would have chosen a different road. All we needed was for someone to realize they'd seen our car one too many times and think we were up to something.

Which we, of course, were.

"Who's still allowed to work?"

Mark shot me a you're-not-going-to-believe-me look.

I leaned my temple against the window. Perfect. "Don't tell me. Rigman, Grady Scherwin, and Quincey."

"Lawrence is still there, too, but he and Quincey have been put on traffic. If they're caught accessing files, it'll mean their jobs. Erik said the only reason they kept Lawrence and Quincey on at all was because they wouldn't have been able to cover all the shifts otherwise."

This had to be some kind of a twisted joke. Of the fourteen officers who *weren't* dead or missing, ten had been removed from duty because of their connections to Mark. In a way, that spoke more highly of Mark than almost anything else.

But it left us with two bad options.

We either couldn't get the file that looked like it held the key to all of this. Or we had to play Russian roulette with who to trust.

Mark made another right turn. We drove past Quantum

Mechanics.

"What about one of the dispatchers?" he asked. "When they're working the desk, they're often asked to pull a file for someone. It wouldn't look suspicious. Aren't you friends with Sheila?"

I held back a flinch. "Sheila wasn't willing to even give me a name when I wanted to know who was working the night Troy died. Both Henry and Case would require us to lie to them. And, at this point, I'm not sure they'd buy it. If I was accessing that file officially, I wouldn't need to ask one of them to get it for me. Neither would you. We'd get it from Detective Dillion."

Henry might still do it. He hadn't seemed to care so much about whether I was telling him the truth or not as long as he had a story he could tell to cover his hind end if anyone asked. That also meant he'd likely turn us in without resistance to save himself if it came to that, though.

"I think we should ask Rigman," I said at the same time as Mark said, "I think we should ask Scherwin."

I'd rather smooch a creepy, crawly forest creature than ask Grady Scherwin for help. "Really? Grady Scherwin?"

"The only reason you don't want to ask Scherwin is you don't like him," Mark said.

My inner child wanted to cross her arms and pout at the implication, but that would only prove his point. "You don't like him, either."

"I don't, but this isn't about who we like or don't like. It's about who we think is least likely to have been involved in the corruption going on."

I slumped back in my seat. Grady Scherwin was a jerk, but

did that mean I thought he was also a dirty cop? Just because someone was a police officer and followed the rules didn't necessarily mean they also had to be a nice person. "Let's each make our case, then. You said yourself that Scherwin is badge-heavy. He likes power. He'd probably love to be controlling everything behind the scenes and congratulating himself on how he's getting away with it."

Mark was shaking his head before I even finished. It hit my nerves about as well as wet shoes squeaking on a linoleum floor. It made me feel like he hadn't listened to everything before deciding I was wrong.

I also knew that Mark always listened, even when it appeared like he wasn't. Now wasn't the time to pick a fight over something unrelated.

Mark pulled into the animal shelter parking lot. He must have finally realized, too, that we couldn't keep driving by the police station without drawing attention. "Grady likes respect. He likes exercising his authority as an officer because it publicly gives him that respect. Shady backroom deals aren't going to give him the kind of validation he's looking for."

He had me there. "Okay, but Grady Scherwin grew up here, and he's been with the Fair Haven PD longer than Rigman. I've had plenty of opportunities to study the pictures in the lobby."

One of the walls in the lobby of the Fair Haven police department was lined with a picture taken on January second of each new year. I'd looked at them multiple times over the past months while I waited for Elise or Erik or whoever else I'd come to meet or talk to.

Assuming I remembered correctly, the people who'd been

there before Wilson took over as chief were Lawrence, Quincey, Grady Scherwin, Henry McCloud, Case Hammond, and the chaplain. Elise and Rigman had joined shortly after, when a couple of the older officers must have retired. Everyone else filled in the gaps along the way.

"Rigman grew up here, too," Mark said. "He only worked on another force waiting for a spot to open here. He wouldn't be in the picture the year Chief Wilson took over because it was taken a month or two before Rigman got hired. He was here that year. I know because he beat Elise out for the spot."

That was suspicious timing. So was that Rigman would have waited so long for a job "back home" only to decide later on in his career that he wanted to make a change and specialize in crime scene reconstruction, a job that would likely move him to a bigger city. Maybe he saw that he was about to get caught, and he was ready to close up what he was doing in Fair Haven and move on.

"What if they're both involved?" I asked softly.

Mark went gray around the lips. "Then we're screwed."

We had to take a risk on one of them. We needed to see what was in that case file that the killer wanted to hide so badly. "I don't suppose saying Grady Scherwin makes my skin crawl would change your mind?"

Mark's dimples peeked out. "The opposite, actually. I think whoever managed to run this scheme for this long has better people skills than Grady Scherwin."

Point taken. The best deceivers were usually charming or forgettable. Grady Scherwin was neither.

"You win. Grady Scherwin it is."

18

*W*e decided to grab take-out fish and chips from A Salt & Battery before we headed to the police station to wait for shift change. Grady Scherwin would either be coming into work or heading home from work since they were short-handed. It was the best time to catch him. Neither of us knew where he lived or had his cell phone number.

I paid for our meals, since Mark forgot his wallet at my house, and we ate in the car parked out front of A Salt & Battery. It would have been warmer inside, but neither of us felt like facing the stares Mark would get.

Nearing the end of his meal, Mark yawned again large enough that his jaw looked like it was going to fall off his face.

I crumpled up my now-empty container and shoved it back into the plastic bag it came in. I tossed it into the back seat, next to my purse. "Are you sure you don't want to wait until tomorrow?"

"I'll be fine. Just didn't sleep well the last few nights." Mark clamped a hand over his mouth, but the twist to his features gave it away that he was yawning again. "We need to do this tonight. Our wedding is coming fast. I can't leave the country anymore, so we've already lost our honeymoon. And we don't know what else this guy has planned."

I'd completely forgotten that I was supposed to go into the dress shop sometime today to try on my dress again. Between my late, then sleepless, night with Isabel, Mark getting out on bail today, and the pieces we'd fit together since then, it'd gotten pushed to the back of my mind.

But marrying Mark and getting to spend the rest of our lives together was the important part, not what I wore to get married. The priority was this case. "At least let me drive then."

He handed over the keys without an argument. He must be exhausted. Mark was easily the better driver of the two of us, especially on winter roads.

We swapped seats, and I drove us down to the Fair Haven police station, going around the back side into the parking lot normally reserved for staff. Unlike much of Fair Haven, street lights lit the parking lot. I picked the corner with the most shadows, in order to wait. With our luck lately, Detective Dillion would come out before we spotted Grady Scherwin. Then we'd have some real explaining to do.

Mark and I fell into silence, and the clock on my dashboard ticked another minute closer to shift change. The staff coming in should be arriving soon, slightly before the staff leaving.

I sent up a small prayer that Grady would arrive alone rather than at the same time as another staff member.

A truck with wheels almost as tall as I was rolled into the

parking lot, a low rumble ensuring everyone knew it was a diesel engine. The driver pulled up almost directly under one of the street lights. He took two spots, angling his truck so that no one could park too close. The driver had to be a man—no woman I knew felt the need to drive a truck like that.

Maybe it was because I was from Washington, DC, where parking spots were at a premium, but people who took up two spaces to protect their paint job was one of my pet peeves.

The door opened, and Grady Scherwin stepped onto the running boards and then down to the ground. I couldn't see his sandy blond buzz cut under his beanie, but the physique was right—body-builder arms and a gut that said he needed more cardio and less weight training.

The fact that he didn't climb back in upon seeing that he was taking up two spots made it clear he'd intended to do it. It figured. Just when I thought I couldn't like him any less, he dropped even lower in my estimation. And it had to be right before I needed to ask him a favor.

Mark already had his door open. I scrambled out after him.

Grady parking under the street light would highlight us for anyone else coming or going, but at least his massive truck should partly obscure us. His driver's-side door faced away from the door into the building. And the truck was taller than any of us.

Mark called his last name—just loud enough to be heard, but not loud enough to draw attention from anyone inside.

Grady stopped and turned back. The light shining down on his face emphasized his brow line and cast shadows over his eyes, making it almost impossible for me to gauge his expression.

"Cavanaugh," he said.

He tossed a glance in my direction, but other than that, he didn't acknowledge me. If I hadn't been sleep deprived, I might have been thinking clearly enough to realize it would have been better had I stayed in the car. Instead, I did the second-best thing and hung back.

"I won't hold you up long," Mark said. "But I need you to grab a file for me. My copy somehow disappeared."

Grady leaned against his fender. "I thought you were off until all this gets cleared up."

A warm little bubble that felt an awful lot like softening bloomed in my chest. Grady's tone implied he was sure it would all get sorted and Mark would be back to work.

Now came the moment of truth. Mark would have to ask him directly for the file. If Grady were involved in the corruption scheme, he'd know we were too close to be allowed to continue. I tried to watch him without making it obvious I was watching him.

Mark shoved his gloveless hands in his pockets, and I tamped down on a cringe.

Don't go all Oliver Twist asking for seconds now, I silently coached him. *He needs to see you as an equal.*

"I am, but Chief McTavish asked me to look into something for him. I think the file he gave me could have something to do with his disappearance and what happened to Troy. If I can get that file back and examine it, I'm hoping I can figure out what."

Grady Scherwin crossed his beefy arms over his chest. "You wouldn't be asking me for help if you could get the file some other way. That makes me think the detective doesn't want you to have it."

"We didn't ask him." Mark shifted his weight from one foot to the other. "But you're right. He probably wouldn't have given me the file if I had."

Headlights streamed across us, and I barely stopped myself from instinctively turning my face away like I had something to hide. Sheila climbed out of the newly arrived car. The way she ducked her own head told me she'd seen me, but was trying to pretend like she hadn't so she didn't have to come over and say hello.

Grady's gaze shifted slightly in her direction. "My shift's about to start."

I had to do something before he not only walked away, but also went straight to Detective Dillion and told him what we were up to.

I moved in close to Mark, my body angled slightly away from Grady. "Come on," I said in a whisper I was sure was loud enough for Grady to still catch. "I told you he wouldn't care about trying to get Chief McTavish back."

The look he gave me was the facial equivalent of flipping me the middle finger. "I'm the only one around here who seems to think the chief's still alive. I've been going door-to-door on my own time, trying to find leads."

That warm little bubble in my chest tried to expand. It showed a lot of loyalty if he were telling the truth. It also showed me the button to push.

I replied with a *yeah, right* look. "If that was true, you'd help us."

Grady very deliberately turned his focus from me to Mark, as if by ignoring me he could make me disappear. "I'll help, but I want something in return."

Such a caring altruist, I felt like saying. Instead, I bit the inside of my cheek to keep quiet.

"Like what?" There was enough wariness to Mark's voice to let Grady know it wasn't a lock. Mark wasn't desperate enough to give him anything. There'd still be limits.

"I'm going to be doing you a favor," Grady said. "I want a favor."

Mark's arms straightened by his sides, like his elbows locked on him. "What kind of a favor?"

"Not from you." He swung his gaze in my direction. "From her. Sometime when I need it."

That growing warm bubble popped, leaving a dark gap in its place. He wanted to know he had me in his debt, whether as payback or ego. Jerk.

But it didn't matter. We needed that file. "As long as it's within legal and moral boundaries, I'll owe you one."

The words tasted bitter and gritty coming out.

Mark explained to Grady what he was looking for.

Grady hooked a thumb in the direction of our car. "I'll bring the file to you."

Another car pulled in as we parted ways. Mark and I kept our pace easy and slow like we weren't worried about being seen.

"Thank you," he whispered. "I know that couldn't have been easy."

Promising hadn't been as bad as fulfilling would be when the urgency had passed and I had to deal with Grady Scherwin holding it over my head that I owed him.

Mark and I climbed back into the car, and I started it to keep us warm. Snow drifted down in heavy flakes, looking like diamonds in the halos of light cast around the street lamps.

Sitting here with Mark would be almost romantic if it weren't for why we were here. It was the kind of night where the snow would continue to get heavier, and the best place to be was somewhere safe and warm with hot chocolate, watching it fall.

Ten minutes passed with two more people arriving. Finally, the door of the station opened and two men came out. The rollover belly gave Grady away, but I couldn't identify the other man.

If he'd betrayed us to Detective Dillion...

They moved under a street light, and Henry's profile came into view. He raised a hand in goodbye and parted from Grady.

Another uniformed officer came out of the door shortly after them. We couldn't have picked a busier place to conduct a transaction we wanted to keep secret if we'd picked the main terminal at a major airport.

Grady strode straight for us. I rolled down the window.

He handed me a sheaf of papers. "I wasn't going to take the original. I photocopied it for you."

"Everything okay here?" a man's voice said from behind Grady.

Brandon Rigman stepped up beside Grady into that I'm-here-if-you-need-me distance. Close enough he could have easily seen that Grady handed me something. I dropped the papers down between the door and my seat and brought both hands up to the edge of the window. Hopefully, if he had thought he saw Grady give me papers, he'd think he'd been mistaken when he saw my empty hands. Though it made for an awkward looking posture from me.

"Yeah. Everything's fine." Grady stepped back away from the car. "Mark accidentally left his belt behind when he checked out his personal items earlier today. I told him I'd look for it."

The man was a good liar. Granted, many police officers were since they often had to lie to criminals, but it didn't instill confidence in me that he wasn't playing us. He could still be the guy. If he wasn't, Rigman was.

And now they both might know we had the file.

I held my breath until Rigman and Grady walked away, going their separate directions, and I pulled out of the Fair Haven police department parking lot.

Mark looked down at his chest. "I'm going to need more clothes."

The regret in his voice made me think he didn't want to go back to his house for them. I couldn't blame him. I didn't want to return there, either, even after the crime scene clean-up team did their work. But he hadn't brought anything with him to Elise and Erik's house because the police hadn't allowed him to remove anything from his home. Thankfully, he'd already moved a lot of his belongings into my place in preparation for our wedding.

"We can go to my house to get some of the clothes from there, and then I'll bring you back to Elise's."

"Have I told you lately that I love you?"

He had, but I had a feeling I'd never get tired of hearing it.

I changed my signal light, and instead of turning right and heading directly for Elise and Erik's, I took the right turn onto the gravel road leading to Sugarwood.

The dark-colored car behind me made the right turn as well even though it'd been signaling to go left.

My heart felt like it hit the bottom of my throat and then tumbled down into my stomach.

"I'm trying not to be paranoid and panicky." My voice said the opposite of my words. "But I think we're being followed."

19

"What?" Mark twisted in his seat and looked out the back window. "Are you sure?"

I explained to him what I'd seen. "It must be Grady Scherwin. The car could be an unmarked police cruiser."

"Grady wouldn't have a reason to follow us. He knows what we have and why we have it. It's more likely Rigman."

"What would Rigman gain from following us?" Oh crap. There was another option for who it could be. "It might be Isabel's husband."

Mark was still watching the car behind us. "Isabel our cupcake designer?"

A lot had happened while he was in jail and I couldn't talk to him. I caught him up as quickly as I could. "If he's the one following us, he's trying to find out where Isabel is hiding. I can't lead him back to my house."

Mark groaned. "Let's take care of two problems at once. Make the next turn. I'll watch to see if the car continues to follow us, and we'll be heading away from Sugarwood just in case it is Isabel's husband."

I slowed to take the turn. My car fishtailed slightly on the snow-covered road despite my caution. The car behind gained on us.

I made the turn and accelerated again. Trees bordered the left side of the road, and a deep ditch lined the right. Even with the bright moonlight, I could barely make out the shoulders of the road under the snow.

Hopefully Mark knew where this road would take us because I didn't. I hadn't had a reason to travel the back roads in this direction before now.

"Still there," Mark said.

I glanced in my rearview mirror. Still there and getting closer. Whoever it was didn't seem to care anymore if we knew he was following us.

That couldn't mean anything good.

My heart felt like it was pounding too high in my chest. "Maybe you should call the police."

Mark reached into his jacket pockets, then patted the pockets of his jeans. "I left my phone in the plastic bag on your counter with my wallet and everything else." His voice sounded hollow. "I thought we'd head straight back after grabbing the file from my place."

The car tailgated us now. I picked up my speed slightly. In the moonlight, I couldn't see the driver clearly enough to tell who it was. I wasn't even sure if it was a man or a woman.

I tried to watch the car in the rearview mirror while still

watching the road. The car drew closer, and its front lights disappeared from my view. Almost like it was going to—

The driver hit my car like we were two bumper cars at a carnival. My car jumped forward and skidded to the side. My hands clenched around the wheel, fighting the drag. My foot wanted to slam on the brakes, but I could hear Erik's voice in my head during our winter driving lessons, telling me not to touch my brakes if I was sliding.

I straightened the car out and hit the gas, aiming down the middle of the road to give myself the biggest cushion between the trees and the ditch, praying we wouldn't meet any cars driving in the other direction.

Our only hope was to outrun him. I didn't know much about cars, but I knew mine had great acceleration when I went to pass another vehicle on the highway.

"Where's your phone?" There was a frantic note to Mark's voice, but I could barely hear him over the blood pounding in my head.

I didn't dare take my gaze off the road to look at him. "In my purse. In the back seat."

I caught movement in my peripheral vision.

"I can't reach it without unbuckling," Mark said.

In the mirror, the car gained on us again. I couldn't go any faster or I'd lose control of my car without his help.

"Don't unbuckle." It came out as a half-scream. I swallowed hard. If this was Isabel's husband, it was no wonder she'd run and was terrified of him finding her. "The lunatic's going to ram us again any second."

Instead of crashing into us from behind, he inched up along-side my left fender.

"We need backup," Mark said. "I have to try to reach it."

We did need help, but if whoever this was wrapped us around a tree or crashed us into the ditch, Mark needed to have his seatbelt on more. It was his only chance of surviving. "I'll try to sync the Bluetooth. Siri, turn on—"

The dark car hit us. Metal screeched, and we were spinning. A scream filled my ears—too high-pitched to belong to Mark.

And then we were falling.

20

The next thing I remembered, I was dangling, suspended by my seatbelt, my arms partly hanging beneath me, partly resting on a nylon material covered in a white powder. Deployed airbag?

My whole body had a flu-like ache to it, and the right side of my face throbbed. Except my feet. They felt wet and so cold they hurt almost more than the rest of me combined.

Where were we? My mind struggled to focus and figure out what was going on.

The chase and crash came back in bits and pieces.

We had to be nose-down in the ditch. That also meant my feet felt like an amateur acupuncturist was practicing on them because the front of my car sat in water. Thank the Lord we weren't completely upside-down or Mark and I would have drowned by now.

"Mark?" My voice croaked out.

No answer.

I gingerly turned my head.

He hung next to me, his airbag also deployed. Now I was extra grateful he hadn't taken his seatbelt off to reach for my phone.

"Mark? Are you okay?"

No movement.

My chest suddenly felt like I was on a planet with double earth's gravity. I couldn't get enough air in. *Dear God, please let him not be dead.*

I stretched my arm out as far as I could and touched his lips. Warm breath kissed my fingers. At least he was still breathing.

Tears pressed against my eyes, but I couldn't cry now. Mark needed medical help. I probably did too. With all the adrenaline coursing through me, I could have a broken bone and not know it.

Besides, the person who ran us off the road might still be out there, waiting to see if we'd survived and finish us off if we had.

Even if he wasn't, we couldn't stay hanging here. Isabel would eventually worry about me when I didn't come home, but that could be hours from now, and she wouldn't know who to call. She might be too afraid to call the police, and she didn't have Elise or Mark's mom's phone number.

If she did manage to convince people to look for us, they wouldn't look here. This wasn't a road we normally traveled. My car might not even be visible from the road. The ditch was probably ten to twelve feet deep.

We couldn't survive the night out here with our feet swimming around in sub-zero water. I couldn't even turn on my car to warm us up. It'd stopped running sometime during the crash.

Assuming it would even start at this point, it might not be safe to try. It might have a fuel leak.

Tony at Quantum Mechanics should give me a bulk discount for all the business I brought him. I'd need it with how my insurance rates were sure to go up. This car wasn't even a year old.

Focus. I had to focus. I couldn't let my panic-brain lead me down unimportant rabbit trails.

Right before the crash, I'd been trying to call for help. That still seemed like the smartest move.

The problem was I couldn't use Bluetooth anymore. With my car off, my phone wouldn't connect. I'd have to find my phone and make the call manually. Which all depended on my phone not being underneath the water flooding the front of my car. And on me being able to get out of my seatbelt without breaking something or tipping the car over.

Take one thing at a time, as my mom would say.

"Siri, can you hear me?" I felt a little silly talking to my phone. I'd never used the voice interface for anything other than turning on Bluetooth before.

"I'm sorry," an automated woman's voice replied. "I didn't catch that."

Thank God. My phone was still above water.

It'd sounded like it'd come from directly behind me. On top of me, really. My purse could be balanced on the back of my seat.

I reached around above me, but I couldn't get my fingers far beyond the edge of my seat. I wasn't going to be able to reach my purse while buckled in.

Mark groaned beside me. "What happened?"

His voice was weak, but his words were clear. Hopefully that meant he didn't have a serious head injury.

"Stay still. We're in a ditch. I'm trying to get my phone."

Mark groaned again, but it had a different tone to it. "I was hoping that was a nightmare. Is he still out there?"

"No way to tell."

I had the uncomfortable suspicion that he was, but that he'd rather leave this looking like an accident. If we died in this ditch, no one would suspect it was anything other than a tragic accident. My unfortunate accident history would play right into it.

I had to get my phone before he decided to check. With the kind of accident we'd had, the medical examiner who did our autopsies might not spot the difference between crash injuries and the crowbar that finished us off.

I couldn't simply release my seatbelt. I'd smash down into my steering wheel and probably break my ribs. My upper body wasn't strong enough to support me and prevent a fall, even if I hadn't needed one hand to release the seatbelt.

Maybe I could get my knees up so I could balance on the steering wheel while I released the belt.

I pulled up one knee, but I hit the steering wheel. It wasn't going to fit in the space between the seat and the wheel. Maybe I could swing my leg around the wheel.

I braced my hands against the wheel and swung my knee out to the side.

Something swished against my leg in the water. I lowered my leg and glanced down. Paper?

Oh no. I'd slid the photocopy of the file Grady gave us next to my seat. It must have come loose in the crash.

It wasn't even like the water was clean. After soaking in muddy ditch water, it'd be unreadable.

Though if we didn't survive, it wouldn't matter.

I drew my knee up beside the wheel again. This would be easier if I did yoga instead of riding a bike. Then I'd be flexible with lean legs.

I wriggled around, but I couldn't get it into position. It wasn't going to work. The positioning of the wheel, the seat, and my body wouldn't allow me to bring my legs into a position to help support me at all.

I tried to relax and think, but the seatbelt cut into my skin. Each breath seemed to take a bit more effort than the one before, with all my weight hanging off my waist and chest.

I had to think. My phone couldn't make a call through my car with the car turned off. Maybe I could still send a text using my voice. I hadn't tried it before, and no one I knew regularly used the feature. But my phone could do it, couldn't it? I thought I'd seen it on a commercial.

The best person to text seemed to be Erik. He'd take my text seriously and act swiftly, but he wouldn't panic. I wouldn't know if the text went through, and I wouldn't be able to respond to any questions Erik had, so I'd have to be perfectly clear the first time.

"What road are we on?" I asked Mark. "And the crossroads as best as you can remember."

He gave me the names.

I thought about crossing my fingers, but that wouldn't help anything. Instead I sent up a quick prayer that this would work.

"Siri, tell Erik *I was run off Brookside, between Green and Willowvale. I need help.*"

"Okay," the automated voice said. "Telling Erik *I was run off Brookside between Green and Willowvale. I need help.* Is this what you want to say?"

"Yes," I nearly shouted.

"Sending."

I tried to listen for the little swish sound that signaled a text had sent, but my purse muffled it too much.

Hopefully this wasn't a dead zone. If it was, the text would sit in limbo until my phone reached a spot with service. If nothing else, if we didn't make it out of this, my text would tell Erik this hadn't been an accident.

It wasn't as good as calling 911, but it was the best we had.

My teeth chattered. The chill was starting to feel like it came from the inside rather than just the outside. "How long can we afford to wait to see if he got it?"

"Ten minutes," Mark said. "The water's too cold. After that, the guarantee of hypothermia will outweigh the risk of making our injuries worse by unbuckling and letting ourselves fall."

21

I pressed the light button on my watch again. The face glowed bluish-green, illuminating the numbers.

"What are we at?" Mark asked.

"Nine minutes."

I brushed my fingers against my seatbelt. I'd give Erik every second of the ten minutes to send help for us. I'd need that time to brace myself anyway. There was no way this wasn't going to hurt if I dropped from my suspended position.

The seconds ticked away. My watch light clicked off again a few seconds before we hit the ten-minute point.

I sucked in a long breath. "I'll go first. I have a shorter distance to fall."

"Wait." Mark reached out toward me. "I think I hear them."

I strained my ears. It was faint but...yes. Sirens. And they were coming toward us.

THE WHOLE CAVANAUGH CLAN WAS ALREADY WAITING WHEN WE reached the hospital—a side effect of texting Erik. If I'd ever doubted that I was already considered a member of the family, I didn't anymore. They didn't flock only to Mark. They flocked to me as well, fussing and asking questions. The doctors had to order them to move back and wait.

For the next few hours, they shuttled me around to have x-rays and CT scans and other exams that I was too tired to track. Elise went back and forth between me and Mark, updating each of us on the other.

The positive side was that the results all came back clean. I sent up my millionth *Thank you, Lord* prayer. I'd seen less serious accidents result in broken backs and death. Mark had a concussion and a dislocated shoulder. I'd be bruised and sore, but I was okay.

Assuming you could call having a shiner two weeks before your wedding *okay*. I'd caught a glimpse of myself in a piece of reflective metal as they'd wheeled me from one test to another. The air bag must have hit me in the face. I had a black eye, a cheekbone already sporting a bruise, and a few scrapes. Better that, though, than the steering wheel catching me in the face.

When they finally brought me back to the room where they wanted to keep me overnight for observation, Detective Dillion sat in the chair next to my bed.

"I hope you don't mind." He propped one foot up on the opposite knee in the way some men had of crossing their legs. "I asked your family to wait until I'd spoken to you."

I did mind. There was no reason some of the Cavanaughs

couldn't be with me while I gave him my statement. But I had the distinct impression that he didn't actually care.

The nurse helped me settle into the bed and gave me a look that said *Should I make him leave?*

I smiled in a way that I hoped let her know I was fine. He needed to take my statement before he could hunt down who'd done this. As much as he irked me, I wanted him to be able to do his job.

"The call button's here"—the nurse pointed to it—"in case you need *anything*."

Detective Dillion watched her go, an annoyed look on his face like she should have realized he was the good guy and I was the one engaged to a criminal. "I'm sure you're ready with a statement to give me about what happened, but I wanted to be sure before you did that you realize we'll protect you if this was an attempted murder-suicide by Cavanaugh. You don't have to lie to protect him because you're afraid of what he'll do."

Wow. This man was one hundred percent convinced that Mark was a villain. "I was driving, so I can guarantee that wasn't the case. You can confirm that with the first responders if you'd like."

He took down my statement without further jabs at Mark. Any time I tried to stray into why we might have been run off the road, though, he shut me down. Which was probably for the best anyway. I couldn't have elaborated on the possible reasons without mentioning the file, and if I wanted another copy, I couldn't let Detective Dillion know how we'd acquired the copy we had.

Elise came into the room as I was finishing. Her patience with Detective Dillion isolating me must have finally run out.

He vacated the chair next to my bed, and she dropped into it and shot a look at Detective Dillion's retreating back that said she'd love it if he kept on walking, straight out of Fair Haven. "If we can't find Chief McTavish, I hope they don't stick us with him permanently."

I doubted Detective Dillion would be willing to stay even if they asked him. "Has everyone else gone home?"

Elise nodded. "Everyone but Erik and me. We're going to sleep here. Just in case."

Just in case whoever ran us off the road came back to kill us while we slept. That seemed unlikely. They'd wanted our crash to look like an accident. Otherwise, they could have climbed down into the ditch and shot us both while we dangled from our seatbelts like laundry on the line.

That said, I'd sleep better knowing Elise was here, just like Isabel had slept better in my house than she had in her truck.

Elise leaned back in her chair and then shifted around as if she were trying to find the most comfortable position to take a cat nap. "Erik wanted me to make sure you knew for future reference that your phone will dial 911 if you tell it to even if it isn't connected to Bluetooth."

That would have been useful information to have a couple of hours ago. That's what I got for avoiding the voice functions on my phone because the automated voice gave me the willies. Mark might have thought of it if he didn't have a head injury, but I hadn't even realized the option existed.

"As soon as I have a chance at the Internet, I'm going to

research everything my phone can do with voice commands. Hopefully that will mean I never need to use them."

Elise laughed. "Is there anything else you need before I get too comfortable?"

That didn't seem like a real risk considering she planned to sleep in a hospital chair. But I did need to call Isabel and warn her that her husband might be in Fair Haven so she should lie low at my house for now. If it had been her husband, he clearly didn't know where she was hiding since he'd been following me. She should be safe at my house overnight.

I also needed to get us another copy of that file as soon as possible. My credit with Grady Scherwin had run out, but Elise might still have some luck.

EMS had rescued my purse from my car and Elise had it, so I called Isabel first. I got the impression that this wasn't the first time he'd found her. And that she would have been gone tonight if she hadn't felt responsible for returning my kindness of a place to sleep by watching my dogs while I was in the hospital.

We disconnected the call, and I laid my phone down on the bed beside me.

I placed a hand over top of it. As silly as it was, I felt better being able to reach out and touch it and know that it was there. "Now I need you to call Grady Scherwin for me."

Elise rolled her eyes. "Funny."

I wished I was joking. I caught her up on what Mark and I had been doing right before the crash. There hadn't been the time or the privacy before now.

Elise's skin took on the pale, translucent quality of tracing paper. "Grady Scherwin it is. I'll have to call the station, though. I don't have his personal number, either."

I'd have wondered about her if she did.

Elise dialed. "Hey, Sheila." Her foot tapped a rhythm on the floor. "I need to get ahold of Grady, and I know he's working tonight. Could you give me his cell number or get in touch with him yourself to have him call me right away? It's important."

She hadn't needed to tell Sheila her name. The dispatchers really must get to know the officers' voices well.

I could hear Sheila saying something on the other end, but I couldn't make out the words.

Elise's gaze skittered in my direction. "Are you sure?" she asked into the phone.

More noise on the other end.

Elise's lips moved in what might have been a silent curse word. "Thanks, Sheila."

She disconnected the call.

A tension headache built at the base of my skull. "What's wrong?"

"Grady was put on administrative leave. Effective immediately. Sheila gave me his cell phone number but…"

But we wouldn't need it. If Grady had been relieved of duty, too, he couldn't get us another copy of the file.

My ruse to hide the papers from Rigman must have failed. It had to have been him, both who ran us off the road and who reported Grady to keep him away from the file going forward on the off chance we survived. Perhaps he'd also done it because Grady had shown loyalty to Chief McTavish by searching for him during his off hours. Someone who would do that might have examined the file himself if Mark and I had died in that crash.

We might never know Rigman's full reasons unless he confessed once we had solid evidence against him.

His reasons didn't matter as much as proving his guilt, though. We had to get that file.

Unfortunately, there was only one man left who could give it to us—Detective Dillion.

22

*E*lise insisted on grabbing a wheelchair even though I told her I could walk to Mark's room. We needed to catch Detective Dillion before he left. He could already be done taking Mark's statement.

Once he left the hospital, our chances of convincing him to allow us to see the file shrunk significantly. Asking him over the phone—assuming he'd even take our call—had the same odds of success as I had of becoming a prima ballerina. I also doubted we'd be able to convince him to come back and speak with us.

Elise rolled me down the hall so fast we got a dirty look from a nurse and a personal support worker.

Detective Dillion was coming out of Mark's room as we rolled up.

"Change your mind?" he asked.

"About Mark causing the accident? Nope."

The wheelchair twitched underneath me like Elise's hands

had spastically closed on the handles. She clearly hadn't realized the detective hoped to pin that on Mark as well.

I placed a hand on one wheel. "But you said if I thought of a reason anyone might have wanted to kill us, I should let you know."

He let out a this-better-not-be-a-waste-of-my-time sigh and swept a hand toward the door.

Elise pushed me in, and Detective Dillion followed us. Mark raised an eyebrow. Elise scooted around the bed and whispered in his ear.

Detective Dillion couldn't have failed to see it, but Mark shouldn't be blindsided by what was coming. He nodded at me. I took it as a *go for it*.

At this point, we didn't really have anything to lose.

Detective Dillion stayed near the doorway, leaning on the wall with his arms crossed.

Elise spun me around to face him better like she'd read my mind.

"Mark has been helping Chief McTavish investigate a corruption ring that former Chief Wilson was a part of. Chief McTavish gave Mark a file on the death of Chief John Zacharius, the man Wilson took over the role of police chief from. Chief McTavish felt Chief Zacharius' death was connected somehow. The file was stolen from Mark's house the night Troy Summoner was killed."

Detective Dillion made an exaggerated show of checking his watch. "I don't have time to listen to you argue why I shouldn't have arrested Cavanaugh for Officer Summoner's murder."

Of course not, I wanted to say. *Heaven forbid you might have to admit you arrested the wrong man.*

But I didn't, because if we could get a copy of the file, it might give us the evidence to prove Mark's innocence strongly enough to force the district attorney to drop all charges before the case went to trial. At that point, Detective Dillion's opinion wouldn't matter.

"I told you all that because we got another copy of the file shortly before we were run off the road. We believe they did it to stop Mark from seeing whatever was in it."

"And you want me to give you a fresh copy?"

The tone of his voice already said *no way.*

He pushed off the wall. "Can you tell me there's no other possible reason someone would have tried to kill either of you? Because unless you can, I'm not handing confidential material over to a man who stands accused of murder."

I started to say that there couldn't be any other reason. But there could. Isabel's husband for one. Someone else one of us had angered in our past investigations for two and up.

Detective Dillion wagged his head. He must have read it in my expression.

"Cavanaugh will have his day in court. Save your stories for then."

WHEN SHE DROPPED ME OFF AT MY HOUSE THE NEXT AFTERNOON, Elise wanted to stay and make sure I was alright, but I convinced her to go home and see her kids. The truth was that Elise's body language screamed *I'm a cop* even when she was out of uniform. Isabel would take one look at her and escape out a back window if Elise came inside.

Isabel and the dogs met me at the front door. I tried my best to dodge Velma and Toby's whip-like tails as they welcomed me. Taking a blow from their tails hurt on the best of days, and my whole body still felt like I'd fallen out of a second-story window.

I used one hand to pet each dog at the same time. "How did it go with these two last night?"

"They were angels."

My dogs were a lot of things, including sweet and loveable. Angelic, though, wasn't one of them.

One corner of Isabel's mouth twitched like she was trying not to smile. "Mostly. The black-and-white one did eat my dinner. But I did an Internet search to make sure nothing in it would hurt her afterward."

Now that sounded more like my dogs. "Don't feel bad. It's not the first time Velma has been counter surfing."

Toby tried to wedge himself in between Velma and my leg for exclusive welcome-home cuddles. He stepped on a purple duffle bag sitting by the door.

Isabel's bag.

I stretched my hand toward it. "You don't have to leave."

All the smile drained out of her. "I think I do. If Jerrod is here in Fair Haven and knows that you'd be able to lead him to me, it's only a matter of time before he finds me."

Aside from the fact that my wedding would be cake-less if she left now, running off on her own didn't seem like the safest thing to do. "We don't know that it was your husband. I think this attack has to do with Mark's case." I waded through the happy dog mob toward her. "Besides, you're safer here where you have allies and people watching out for you. We can work together. I'll help you get a restraining order."

"That puts you in too much danger. Look what it already might have done." She sidestepped me and the dogs and slung her duffle over her shoulder. "But I want you to know that I appreciate what you did in letting me stay here. Not everyone would have, and it was the best night's sleep I've had in months. When you live in your car, you see too much after dark, even in the nicest towns, to ever feel safe anywhere. I don't so much sleep in my truck as I close my eyes and listen for danger."

You see too much.

For days I'd felt like she wanted to tell me something and yet didn't feel she could or didn't know if she should. She'd been in the vicinity when Chief McTavish was taken. It wasn't only her truck that was there since her truck was her home. And I knew from experience that she would have heard a car pull up—let alone two cars—and she would have been watching.

If she could identify the person who met McTavish that night, we might be able to show that there was a link between his disappearance and the corruption investigation. It could be what we needed to convince Detective Dillion to allow Mark to look at the file. The mastermind behind the corruption cover up in Fair Haven wouldn't have gone to all this trouble if that file wouldn't reveal him.

I spun around. "Did you see something last Thursday night? Two men in the Lakeshore Park parking lot?"

Isabel clenched a hand around her duffle bag strap. Her

knuckles turned pink and white. "Nothing I saw is going to help you. I didn't see faces. I can't identify anyone."

I'd learned with Isabel that what she didn't say was as important as what she did. "Could you identify the cars? Or do you remember a license plate number?"

"Even if I could..." She shook her head.

Even if she could, she couldn't very well give Detective Dillion her fake name. Purchasing a fake ID was a crime.

Reporting what she'd seen to the police would mean her real name showing up in the system as a witness. It could mean testifying at trial. Given what she'd told me about her husband and his law enforcement connections, that was as good as mailing him a letter with her return address on it. She might be able to hide until the trial date, but then he'd be waiting for her.

It was a lot to ask, and yet the stakes for me, for Mark, even for Chief McTavish if he were still alive, were so high.

Maybe there was a way we could both have what we needed.

"Mark and I need the police to allow us to see a file from an old case. We're sure it'll help solve this one. If we could show any sort of connection, it might be enough to convince them. You could tell the police what you know, but do it as an anonymous tip."

Isabel tugged at the zipper on her bag. "My statement isn't going to make the police believe you. It was a member of the police who took your missing man."

A tremor ran up my legs, and I braced a hand against Velma's back for support.

Suspecting something and hearing it confirmed were two

very different situations. When you only suspected, you could still hold out hope you were wrong.

Now I knew. The man behind the corruption cover-up in Fair Haven was also the one who'd kidnapped Chief McTavish, killed Troy, and framed Mark for murder.

And my only hope of proving it lay in convincing a woman who saw the police as an enemy to trust them with her life.

23

I pressed my palms together in a prayer pose. "That's exactly the information I need. Detective Dillion didn't believe us when we told him the investigation Chief McTavish was working on and the recent murder were connected. This might convince him to let us see the file on Chief Zacharius' death. If we find hard evidence in that file, we won't even need your testimony anymore. We'll have enough without it."

At least, that was my theory, but I couldn't let on to Isabel that I was less than completely certain.

She wrapped her hand around the strap of her duffle again like she wasn't sure whether to set it down or walk out the door.

In a way, she and I faced the same challenge. The person we were up against was law enforcement.

Maybe she didn't see that.

I lowered my hands in a sign of surrender, to show her that I had nothing if she walked out. "You weren't able to bring your husband to justice for what he did to you, but you have a chance now to protect other people from a bad cop. Please. Help me."

Isabel's lips lost all their color, and her duffle bag slid off her shoulder. It hit the floor with a thud.

Then she drew her shoulders back into a line that would have made a military drill instructor proud. "You're right. I can't let other people be hurt without anyone to turn to the way I was. I'll tell the detective what I saw."

I CALLED ELISE AND HAD HER AND MARK PICK ISABEL AND ME UP. Fair Haven, unfortunately, didn't have any places that rented cars. Until Tony either fixed mine—which seemed doubtful based on the damage I'd seen once the emergency crews got Mark and me out—or I bought a new one, I was without transportation. Driving there in Isabel's food truck didn't seem advisable in case I was wrong and her husband was the one who ran us off the road. Her truck would point her out to him immediately if he were searching for it.

I filled Mark and Elise in on our way to the police station.

Case Hammond sat behind the front desk, which was actually a relief. I'd been hoping to see either him or Henry. It was going to take a long time before things weren't awkward between Sheila and me.

Elise and Mark took a seat on the bench along the wall, and I marched up to the front desk with Isabel in tow.

"We need to speak to Detective Dillion, please."

Something flickered across Case Hammond's face.

Oh crap. My voice. He thought he recognized my voice. If he put it together that I'd tricked him once before, he might leave us sitting here waiting for Detective Dillion for hours.

Isabel's courage wasn't likely to last that long.

I cleared my throat and tried to make my voice deeper. "It's about Chief McTavish's disappearance. It can't wait."

Isabel moved just enough that her sleeve brushed mine. She must have caught what I was doing with my voice. She wouldn't know why, but I had to be careful not to freak her out, either.

Case glanced at the phone on the desk, then looked over my shoulder.

Footsteps came up behind me.

"Is this for real?" Case asked.

I almost answered him until I realized he was talking to the person behind me. I shifted position. Elise stood off to my right.

"It's for real," she said. "And important enough to call him in if he's not here."

I wanted to hug Elise. She'd spotted something I hadn't. Case had been trying to decide if it was worth the risk to his job to disturb Detective Dillion. With how officers were dropping like bugs in a room full of Raid, I couldn't really blame him for thinking he'd be next if he seemed to be giving us any special treatment.

But he'd worked with Elise. He trusted her in a way that he never would have trusted me. For not the first time, I was grateful for the friendships I'd made since coming here.

He picked up the receiver and dialed a number. "Take a seat," he said to me.

Isabel sat beside me, but she folded and unfolded her hands.

Finally, she trapped them between her knees. She looked more nervous than I'd felt in the past in a courtroom.

Fifteen minutes passed. The front doors swung open, and Detective Dillion entered, dressed in a dark cable-knit sweater and jeans, a scarf and overcoat draped over his arm. He looked almost normal and approachable dressed like that.

He jabbed a finger at me, then at the door to Chief McTavish's office.

If a person could have storm clouds over their heads the way cartoon characters did, he had them. This was off to a great start.

I put a hand under Isabel's elbow in case she decided to bolt and brought her along with me.

Detective Dillion slammed the door to the office behind us. The walls next to it rattled. "This is my first day off since I ended up in this godforsaken place."

I peeked in Isabel's direction. I'd expected her to have a rabbit-face-to-face-with-a-hunter expression. Instead she showed as much emotion as a blank wall. It was almost like she'd disconnected from her body and the situation.

I nudged her gently toward one of the chairs, and she obediently sat. I took the other one.

When I'd dealt with former Chief Wilson and Chief McTavish, I'd settled in and crossed my legs to let them know I wasn't leaving until I got results. I'd been almost cocky.

All the instincts I'd developed for dealing with police officers and prosecuting attorneys while working alongside my parents told me I needed to take the opposite tactic with Detective Dillion.

I demurely crossed my ankles and folded my hands in my lap.

"I know that you're here in part to figure out what happened to Chief McTavish. I knew you'd want any information, even if it came from me. Or if I was the one to find a witness."

Detective Dillion dropped his coat and scarf on the desk. He leaned one elbow on the back of his chair. "I also know a lot about you. Bringing me information to help in the search for Owen McTavish won't earn your fiancé any special favors."

For a second I thought I felt Isabel's gaze on me, but when I looked in her direction, she was staring at the legs of the desk.

I couldn't let Detective Dillion cast doubt on my motives. "I expect you to investigate Troy Summoner's murder thoroughly and without bias. But I'm also hoping when you hear her statement, you'll reconsider allowing Mark to look at the case file for Chief Zacharius' death. We're willing to do it here in your office with you watching us the whole time."

Detective Dillion cursed. "What is it with you and that file? Fine." He yanked out his chair and dropped into it. He pulled out a pen and pad of paper. "Name?"

Isabel's body stayed glacier-still, but she tilted her chin up. "Anonymous."

Detective Dillion didn't audibly sigh at her, but it was in his every expression as he brought the pen away from the page. "If you're not willing to give your name, how can I be sure you're not making this up? Did she pay you off?"

"The reason I won't give my name is also the reason I saw what happened to the missing police chief."

His pen touched down again. "I'm listening."

"My husband beat me regularly for years. The only way I could escape him was to disappear entirely. I can't even put my name on an apartment lease for fear he'll find me. So I sleep in my truck. That's why I was in the parking lot the night someone in a police cruiser tasered another man and dragged him away."

Detective Dillion's pen slipped across the page. He set it down. "You're sure the kidnapper was the one in the cruiser?"

Isabel nodded.

"Could you describe either man?"

"Their heights. A little about their clothes, maybe." She shook her head. "It was dark."

"Can you describe the other vehicle?"

Isabel might not recognize the question for what it was, but I did. He was testing her. If she described a car that wasn't McTavish's, or if she described a generic vehicle that could have fit hundreds of cars in Fair Haven alone, Detective Dillion would discount her whole story.

Isabel gave her description in an eerily calm voice.

The car she described matched what I remembered about Chief McTavish's personal vehicle. I didn't remember his license plate number, but she gave the first three places. Detective Dillion would no doubt check the first chance he got.

He picked his pen back up and tapped it—point, end, point, end—back and forth.

Then he got up and left the room.

"Does that mean he believes me or not?" Isabel asked.

I wasn't sure. It could go either way, depending on how much Detective Dillion allowed his suspicion of me to influence him.

Isabel and I fell into silence. The time between each tick of the clock above the door seemed to lengthen.

I had to fill the void with something before I took the clock off the wall and yanked its batteries out. "Will you reconsider staying? So many of the officers here are my friends, and they're good people. They'd protect you from Jerrod if he came for you."

"I wish I could. It's been a long time since I've had friends."

She said the word tentatively like she wasn't sure we were friends. Given the fact that I'd broken into her truck a couple of days ago and she'd held me at knife point, I couldn't blame her for questioning it. But the talks we'd had let me know we could be friends if we were given the chance.

"That's why I want you to stay and let us help you."

She scraped a nail into the arm of the chair. "If it turns out Jerrod didn't run you off the road, I'll stay for your wedding like I promised, but then I have to go."

I opened my mouth to protest again, but she shook her head.

"I know you want to help and that you think the police here could keep me safe, but they couldn't follow me around like a protective detail. Jerrod would wait until I'm alone. The only way for me to stay safe is to keep moving. Besides, I've already drawn too much attention to myself here. The town's too small, and I'd be too easy to find."

I had to respect her choice. I couldn't force her.

And she had a point. If you wanted to go unnoticed, Fair Haven wasn't the place to do it. "I hope you'll find a spot where you feel safe staying. You'll be safer if you have friends to watch out for you rather than trying to do it yourself." I couldn't keep a grin from my face. "You'll sleep better, too."

Isabel flashed one of her rare firecracker smiles.

The door swung open, and I jumped in my seat. I'd been so focused on Isabel that I hadn't heard anyone approaching.

Detective Dillion led the way, an oversized manila folder under his arm. Mark limped in behind him.

"Does this mean I can leave?" Isabel asked.

The detective nodded.

"Elise will drive you home," I said.

She didn't wait for anyone to change their minds.

I couldn't imagine how much bravery it'd taken for her to come here. Police stations represented business or friendship for me. They represented something entirely different for her. Since Troy was killed, I'd gotten a taste of what it was like. No one should have to be most afraid of the people who should be keeping them safe.

Dillion dropped the file on his desk. "Pull up close. I'm not wasting resources photocopying the thing again."

Mark took the chair Isabel had left and scooted it forward. He opened the folder.

"I looked over the file after you two were here last time." Dillion lowered himself into his chair as if he were tired of it all. "It looks like a straightforward accident. He was out at his cabin during deer-hunting season. When the paramedics arrived, there were cleaning supplies out on the table. It looked like he was planning to clean his gun."

Mark flipped to the next page, reading so intently I almost thought he was going to bring the papers up to touch his nose.

I wouldn't spot anything out of the ordinary in the autopsy report, so there wasn't a point in me trying to read over his shoulder.

I brought my chair closer anyway. "A police chief should know how to handle a gun safely, don't you think?"

"He should have," Dillion said. "The truth of it is that we can get sloppy because we handle weapons so often. I once investigated a case where an otherwise good officer died because he didn't maintain his weapon and it jammed when he needed it to fire. Things happen."

Mark turned another page. He ran his finger along the typing as if trying to help himself focus.

He removed his hand and slowly lowered the other pages back down.

My mouth went dry and my tongue felt too big to comfortably fit inside. He hadn't found anything out of the ordinary.

Dillion was looking at him now too. "So?"

Mark closed the file. "I would have declared it an accident if I'd been the medical examiner. He had gunshot residue on his skin. That, combined with the angle of the wound, says it was close range, and he was shot from below. You wouldn't expect either of those things if someone else were holding the gun. It did look like his head was tilted back when the shot hit his neck, but that'd be consistent with him falling asleep accidentally with the gun still in his hands."

The chair felt a little wobbly underneath me even though I knew it was solid. We couldn't have been mistaken. Why else would someone have taken the file from Mark's house? Why else would someone have tried to kill us after Grady Scherwin gave us a second copy? Why else would someone have taken Chief McTavish if it wasn't to stop his corruption investigation?

Lightning could strike the same place twice. But we weren't a lightning rod, and my parents had taught me to be extra skeptical of anything that seemed like too much of a coincidence.

"May I see the file?" I asked.

Mark slid it over to me.

I avoided the pictures and the autopsy report. Mark would have caught anything suspicious there, and I didn't need to throw up in front of Detective Dillion.

I read through the officers' reports, but they didn't tell me anything that Dillion and Mark hadn't already. Quincey had been one of the responding officers, along with not-yet-chief Wilson. That combination was likely why Chief McTavish hadn't yet crossed Quincey off his list. The responding officers would have reached the location even before the paramedics, giving them time to stage the scene. For all Chief McTavish knew, they'd been the ones to kill Chief Zacharius and then call it in.

That theory depended on one important element, though.

"Who called it in?"

"Zacharias," Dillion said. "We don't have a recording of it because he called the station here rather than 911, but the dispatcher identified his voice. His statement should be in there somewhere if you want to read it for yourself."

Strange that he wouldn't have called 911, knowing that he was likely bleeding out, but instinct must have kicked in. Or he could have thought his people would send help for him faster.

"The dispatcher was sure it was Zacharias?" Mark asked. "Not someone impersonating his voice?"

The tightness in Mark's tone made me look up from flipping through the pages in search of the dispatcher's statement.

The muscles around Dillion's lips tightened. "Like I said, you can read it for yourself if you don't trust me. He said the person who called in was definitely Zacharius. He recognized the voices of the officers he worked with even when they tried to trick him, so he was confident someone couldn't have deceived him."

A cold band tightened around my throat. I'd heard almost that exact explanation before from Henry when I asked him if someone could have been impersonating Troy.

"I need to see the file again," Mark said.

I handed it over to him. He turned immediately back to the autopsy report.

The tightness in my throat made it hard to swallow. I'd assumed that the person behind the corruption cover up in Fair Haven had to be a police officer, but police officers weren't the only ones with access to everything they would have needed to bribe, bully, and benefit from hiding criminal activity.

A dispatcher was the first one to learn about anything that was reported directly to the police. They could delay sending officers in order to give someone they were working with time to get away. They could approach people with an offer of protection in exchange for a cut. They'd know repeat offenders and who the police suspected, giving them an open pool of people to approach.

And anyone who did stumble upon the cover up would be less likely to suspect them. I hadn't. I'd assumed that only the Fair Haven police officers could be involved. I'd overlooked entirely that Henry had also been here before Carl Wilson became chief.

Henry had seen Grady bringing us the file as well as Rigman. Grady might have even told him what he was doing, thinking Henry was safe.

.

Queasiness washed over me, and I rested my head on my arms on the edge of the desk. Bernice, the woman who cleaned Mark's house, was Henry's wife. She cleaned the police station, too. Because as a dispatcher's wife, she was automatically trusted. Henry wouldn't have needed to break in and risk leaving signs of forced entry at Mark's house. He could have used Bernice's key.

"Zacharius didn't make that call," Mark said. "He couldn't have."

I brought my head up. Mark had released some of the pictures and paperwork from the case file and had turned them around toward Dillion.

Mark pointed to the diagram that noted the deceased's injuries, to a spot on the written report, and to one of the pictures. "The medical examiner's report shows exactly what the bullet damaged as it passed through. Assuming the injuries were recorded correctly, Zacharius couldn't have called in his own accident because he wouldn't have been able to speak."

24

*D*etective Dillion placed a call to the medical examiner who'd been brought in to temporarily replace Mark.

"We need confirmation," he said.

While we waited for the medical examiner to arrive, I walked Dillion through the connections I'd made about Henry. Dillion brought the file across the table to himself and turned to the statement given by the dispatcher who took the call.

"Henry McCloud." He kept staring at the paper like he couldn't believe it. "It's a good thing I'm not a gambling man. When you first started on about this file, I would have bet my house that you were blowing smoke up my a—"

A knock rattled the door.

Dillion rose to his feet. "That'll be my second opinion. You two might as well head home and rest. If he confirms that Zacharius couldn't have made that call, I'll bring McCloud in for a little chat."

Mark and I rose to our feet as well. If we'd been dealing with Chief McTavish, I would have angled to stay, and maybe even listen in, as they questioned Henry. But I got the impression that I shouldn't push my luck with Dillion. "Will you give me a call as a courtesy? It'd be nice to know if you make an arrest so I can stop jumping every time a shadow moves."

Dillion inclined his head just enough that I took it as agreement.

GIVEN RECENT EVENTS, ISABEL AND I DECIDED WE'D BOTH FEEL better if we camped out in my living room overnight with the dogs loose. I gave her the couch since she rarely had the luxury, and I took a sleeping bag on the floor.

I woke up the next morning to my cell phone ringing and Toby breathing his doggie breath in my face. At least he wasn't snoring.

The caller ID on my phone listed the Fair Haven police department. I grabbed it up.

"We've arrested McCloud for the murder of Chief Zacharius," Detective Dillion said. "Unfortunately, he's not confessing to anything, and we don't have enough evidence to charge him with the other crimes."

I shifted position so Toby wasn't breathing on me anymore and stroked his ear. He let out a happy groan.

I couldn't quite bring myself to ask Dillion directly what this meant for Mark. Hopefully he'd understand what I meant. "So what happens next?"

"Well, for what it's worth, you've won me over. I'll call the district attorney and see what I can do about getting the charges against Cavanaugh dropped. I can't make any promises. I made a convincing case the first time around, and the DA might still want to take it to trial."

That's exactly what I'd been afraid of. I thanked Detective Dillion, and he told me that he'd lift the suspension of the regular Fair Haven officers. He promised to call if anything else changed.

Once Elise was back on duty, I was sure I'd be receiving regular updates anyway.

Isabel stretched on the couch behind me. "Good news or bad?"

"A little of both."

I caught her up on what Dillion had said. Last night, I'd told her what we'd figured out about the old case and who we suspected was behind it all. Normally I wouldn't have shared so much with someone outside the police force or my law firm, but her choice to stay or go before my wedding depended on who'd run Mark and me off the road. We could safely say now that it hadn't been Isabel's husband.

Isabel planted her feet on the floor, and both Velma and Toby hopped up. As soon as a human moved around in the morning, they took it as their signal that it was time to eat and go for a walk.

I shifted myself into a sitting position, and every muscle in my body screamed at me. Sleeping on the floor after the accident probably hadn't been the best choice. But at least I'd slept.

"I can take them out if you want," Isabel said.

"That obvious I'm hurting?"

"Not really. I'm just familiar with how bad second-day injuries can feel. Besides"—she scrubbed Velma in the spot that made her back foot come up off the ground and beat the air —"I've always loved dogs, and I can't exactly have one in my food truck. Not even a small one. I'd like to take the chance while I have it."

Part of me wanted to argue with her again about leaving, but she'd made it clear she wasn't going to change her mind.

I crawled to my feet. "I'll get their jackets and leashes if you can feed them."

Isabel retrieved their bowls and filled them. "Jerrod brought home a German Shepherd puppy a few years after we were married. Duke, he named him."

She set the bowls into the custom stands I'd gotten for them so the dogs could eat at a comfortable height.

"I don't know why he did it," she continued, "except he expected a dog would give him complete adoration and obedience. I'd always wanted a dog, so I really didn't care what his reasons were."

She paused, and the slurpy noises of my dogs eating filled the gap.

She watched them with obvious sadness. "It was a mess right from the start. Jerrod got jealous when I paid any attention to Duke. Then around the time Duke was six months old or so, Jerrod hit me and Duke growled at him. Jerrod packed him up in the car and took him to the pound. I wasn't even allowed to cry."

She told the story now without tears, too, but there was an

underlying note that let me know it still hurt her and that she still loved and missed that puppy who'd tried to defend her.

I wish I'd known her then. Maybe I could have convinced her to press charges against her husband for his abuse. Maybe she wouldn't be stuck into the life she had now.

"Anyway," Isabel gave a little shudder like she was trying to shake the memory off, "I'll happily take care of your dogs for you while you rest and recover. You'll actually be doing me a favor."

"It'll more likely be while I try to figure out a way to still link Henry McCloud to my accident, the police officer's murder, and our missing police chief."

"And getting ready for your wedding."

"That too."

Once the dogs finished eating, I snapped Velma's jacket on.

Isabel pointed at Velma's orange vest. "Interesting fashion statement."

I really was a better-safe-than-sorry type of person. "I put them on for deer-hunting season so they couldn't be mistaken for deer while running through the bush. Everyone keeps telling me that all the hunters have gone home now, but I'm waiting another few weeks to be safe."

I expected her to make a comment on how there weren't any black-and-white deer so Velma should be safe no matter what.

Instead, Isabel fingered the edge of the vest. "The past case. The police chief died in a hunting cabin, didn't he?"

I bent over to put Toby's jacket on, and he tried to lick my face. I dodged. His first owner had basically let him smooch her whenever he wanted, but I wasn't as big a fan of doggie drool all over me. One time he'd caught me in the lips.

"Yeah," I said. "The man who was arrested tried to stage it as an accident."

I wasn't following her train of thought. Was she afraid Jerrod might be out there and try to kill her with a rifle, like she'd been accidentally shot?

He didn't strike me as a man who'd kill from a distance. Besides, hunting season was over. There'd be no faking an accident this time of year.

I probably should stop worrying and take the orange vests off the dogs' jackets. They were goofy-looking.

"And the hunting cabins are empty this time of year?" Isabel asked.

Oh, wait. She'd said she couldn't even lease an apartment for fear Jerrod would locate her. Maybe she was thinking of squatting in a hunting cabin over the winter rather than in her truck. Some owners might even give her permission to stay for free and without signing a lease. It wasn't like they'd be renting them out again until the summer tourist season.

I strapped Toby in. I hadn't given up on convincing her to stay as much as I liked to tell myself. "I've heard the cabins only have wood stoves for heat, but if you're okay with that, I'm sure we could find you one."

"It's not that. I was thinking that people are creatures of habit. If the guy behind all that's been going on used a hunting cabin once, he might have used it again to either kill or hold your current police chief. They're isolated, right? It's not like anyone would hear someone calling for help."

Toby caught me with his tongue, but I almost didn't mind. It was a long shot, but her logic was sound.

If Henry were following his past patterns, Chief McTavish might even still be alive. Henry had worked hard to win key people over to his side. He had to know that killing McTavish would only bring more investigators in, and his chances of keeping his clandestine business running would fall to almost zero.

But if he could turn Chief McTavish to his side the way he had former Chief Wilson, he could be assured of being able to continue. Even if he planned to kill McTavish, he would have wanted to strategically choose and place the man who'd become chief instead. That could take time, and as long as Chief McTavish were only missing, not dead, they wouldn't replace him.

"I need to call Detective Dillion."

25

"We found him." Static made Erik's voice cut in and out like he was in an area with poor cellular reception. "He's alive and already named Henry McCloud as the one who kidnapped him. Henry wanted him to implicate Quincey in the corruption investigation and then join him in continuing the underground deals he'd made."

I squeezed Mark's hand and smiled at Isabel. We'd all been waiting together at my house for news since Mark and I were barred from traipsing around in the woods on the search teams due to our injuries.

They found him, I mouthed.

I put Erik on speaker. "Where was he?"

"The old Zacharius cabin. Quincey figured we'd be looking for someplace close enough that Henry could easily get to it and back to town, but that was still isolated. He remembered Chief Zacharius' cabin fitting both those requirements."

It felt fitting somehow that Quincey had been the one to find

Chief McTavish. He'd been on the list of suspects, but this would help clear his name.

"I'll text you when I know more," Erik said.

Mark and I went to separate ends of the room to work on writing our vows, while Isabel played with Velma and Toby to give us some peace.

I'd finished my first draft when my phone dinged.

Henry has confessed to everything and is naming names in exchange for some accommodations when he goes to prison. Claims he took his wife's keys for Mark's place without her knowledge.

Henry could be lying to protect Bernice, but I preferred to think it was the truth. She'd always seemed like a nice lady. While she likely hadn't been completely naïve about what her husband had been doing—she'd have known their bank accounts were fatter than they should be—hopefully she had been ignorant of the murders.

Rigman also under arrest as accomplice.

"You were right," I called to Mark. "About Rigman."

I flipped the paper I'd been writing my vows on face down, and Mark and Isabel came over. I laid my cell phone down so they could also read the texts as they came in.

He's claiming he wanted out. That's why he wanted to leave town. Henry wouldn't let him go unless he did this last job for him.

The "last job" could have been killing Troy, or it could have been running us off the road. I didn't feel the need to have Erik specify exactly what role Rigman had played.

All charges against Mark are being dropped.

I turned my face up and smiled at Mark.

He leaned in and stole a kiss. "I guess we get our honeymoon after all," he whispered.

Our wedding, our honeymoon, and the rest of the life we'd planned.

"Do you have flour and sugar?" Isabel asked.

My brain reeled, trying to make the jump from *honeymoon* to *flour*. "I'm not sure."

Isabel took a sheet of paper off the notepad Mark and I had pulled paper from for our vows. "I'll pick some up just in case."

Mark raised an eyebrow at her the way I wished I could.

She grinned. "You two still haven't picked your cake flavors. I figure we can do two things at once—taste test flavors and celebrate."

"IT'S MY HONOR AND GREAT PLEASURE," OUR PASTOR SAID, "TO introduce you to Mr. and Mrs. Mark Cavanaugh."

The recessional music rolled out from the piano, and Ahanti quickly moved the train of my dress aside so I wouldn't trip on it while Mark and I headed down the aisle. Two more failed attempts with the seamstress had left Mandy up until midnight last night making what alternations she could. The bodice was still a little loose and the hem a little long, but none of that mattered.

Mark and I were finally married.

As we turned to walk about down the aisle, I got a look at all the people who'd come to celebrate with us. We hadn't separated the church into bride's side and groom's side. How could we? So many of the people were here for us both.

Russ sat up front with my parents, in the place I would have given to my Uncle Stan. Erik was with the rest of the Cavanaughs and Elise's children—who were his children now too.

Tony Rathmell and his wife and little Noah dressed in a tiny tuxedo, Dave and Nancy and all the rest of the Sugarwood staff took over two rows. Across from them were Chief McTavish and his wife and the other Fair Haven police officers, including Grady Scherwin—my last-minute invite. Even Sheila had come.

Liz, my hairdresser, and her little boy, Derek. Clement and Darlene Dodd, Anderson Taylor and the other members of our law firm, the friends I'd made volunteering at the Fair Haven animal shelter and in the lost pets' group, and so many others filled out the rest of the church.

I'd come to Fair Haven feeling like I'd lost one of the few people in the world who truly cared about me and in the process gained more than I could have imagined. In giving me Sugarwood, Uncle Stan gave me a chance to figure out what I was good at and who I wanted to be. I'd never consider losing him a good thing, but it brought so much good into my life that I knew he'd have been happy for me.

I came to Fair Haven feeling alone.

I wasn't alone any more.

BONUS RECIPE: NICOLE'S WEDDING CUPCAKES

CAKE:

1/2 cup granulated sugar

5 tablespoons butter, softened

1 teaspoon vanilla extract

1/2 teaspoon maple extract

2 large eggs, at room temperature

1 1/4 cups all-purpose flour

1 1/4 teaspoon baking powder

1/4 teaspoon salt

1/4 cup 2% milk, at room temperature

1/4 cup maple syrup

ICING:

1 cup maple syrup

2 egg whites

1/8 teaspoon cream of tartar

TO MAKE THE CAKE:

1. Preheat oven to 350 degrees, and line 12 muffin cups with cupcake liners.

2. In a large bowl, use the medium speed of your mixer to beat together sugar, butter, vanilla extract, and maple extract for about five minutes.

3. Add eggs one at a time. Beat well after each. (Make sure it looks smooth before you move on.)

4. In a medium bowl, whisk together flour, baking powder, and salt.

5. In a separate bowl, mix together milk and ¼ cup maple syrup.

6. Alternating, add flour mixture and milk mixture to the sugar mixture. Start and end with the flour mixture, and mix well after each addition.

7. Divide the batter evenly between 12 muffin cups.

8. Bake for 18 minutes or until a toothpick inserted into the center comes out clean.

9. Cool in the pan for 10 minutes, then move cupcakes to a wire rack to finish cooling.

TO MAKE THE ICING:

10. While the cupcakes are cooling, prepare the icing by bringing 1 cup maple syrup to a boil in a large saucepan over medium heat on the stovetop. Cook until a candy thermometer reads 120 degrees C, then remove from heat.

11. In a bowl, beat the egg whites until they become frothy and start to turn white. Add cream of tartar and continue to beat until it forms soft peaks.

12. On the medium speed of the mixer, gradually whip the maple syrup into the egg whites. Beat for 3-4 minutes, until stiff peaks form.

13. Ice the cooled cupcakes.

MAKES 12 CUCAKES

LETTER FROM THE AUTHOR

Thank you so much for coming along on the journey of this series with me. I know many of you have grown to love Nicole, Mark, and Fair Haven as much as I do.

Nicole now owes her nemesis Grady Scherwin a favor, and he's going to call it in during the next book in the series when Nicole digs up some bones while planting new trees at Sugarwood.

Book 10 (*Rooted in Murder*) will be available in 2019.

In the meantime, you can continue along with Nicole and Mark in *Slay Bells Ringing: A Murder Mystery Duet*. It's two novellas (short novels) in one book.

In "Unsilent Nights," Nicole and Mark head off on their honeymoon, but things don't go as planned. With Mark sick from a source they can't identify and a fellow passenger who went missing while the ship was in the middle of the ocean, Nicole has more than one mystery to solve.

You can also find out what happens to Isabel next in "Ginger

Dead Man" (the second novella inside *Slay Bells Ringing*.) Nicole's words about helping those who can't help themselves sticks with her, and she ends up investigating the strange death of a homeless man.

If you liked *End of the Line*, I'd also really appreciate it if you took a minute to leave a review. Ratings and reviews help me sell more books (which allows me to keep writing them), and they also help fellow readers know if this is a book they might enjoy.

Love,
Emily

ABOUT THE AUTHOR

Emily James grew up watching TV shows like *Matlock, Monk,* and *Murder She Wrote.* (It's pure coincidence that they all begin with an M.) It was no surprise to anyone when she turned into a mystery writer.

Alongside being a writer, she's also a wife, an animal lover, and a new artist. She likes coffee and painting and drinking coffee while painting. She also enjoys cooking. She tries not to do that while painting because, well, you shouldn't eat paint.

Emily and her husband share their home with a blue Great Dane, seven cats (all rescues), and a budgie (who is both the littlest and the loudest).

If you'd like to know as soon as Emily's next mystery releases, please join her newsletter list at www.smarturl.it/emilyjames.

She loves hearing from readers.

www.authoremilyjames.com
authoremilyjames@gmail.com